*Dedicated to a week
in paradise
with the one
who holds my heart.*

Table of contents

Table of contents 4
Chapter One 1
Chapter Two 6
Chapter Three 15
Chapter Four 33
Chapter Five 46
Chapter Six 57
Chapter Seven 68
Chapter Eight 79
Chapter Nine 88
Chapter Ten 98
Chapter Eleven 109
Chapter Twelve 124
Chapter Thirteen 133
Chapter Fourteen 144
Chapter Fifteen 152
Chapter Sixteen 164
Chapter Seventeen 178
Chapter Eighteen 185
Chapter Nineteen 195
Chapter Twenty 209
Chapter Twenty-One 218
Chapter Twenty-Two 229
Chapter Twenty-Three 235
Epilogue 247
Sneak Peek - It All Began with a Mai Tai 256
Sneak Peek - It All Began with a Wedding 265
H.M. Shander Books 277
Acknowledgements 278
About the Author 280

Chapter One

I pronounced it slowly and deliberately, breaking it down into its syllables—zee-watt-an-eh-oh. Zihuatanejo. It sounded idyllic and relaxing, a place with fragrant florals and an ocean that went on for miles. The perfect place to recharge and reflect on the state of my life.

Surveying the magnificent view from the balcony high above the resort, I made mental plans to explore the pools and restaurants right after a hearty breakfast and a lengthy nap on the beach. But first, I scrawled out a note to my best friend Camille, the one I'd convinced only forty-eight hours ago how desperately we needed a girls' vacation. And now we were three thousand miles from home, with no work, and no one to answer to. It was heavenly.

Each exhaled breath pushed out the crappy, wintery air and each long inhale filled my lungs with warm, salty ocean air that held more promises than a child begging her parents for a puppy.

I reread the note to Camille.

Hey lazybones,
If you get this after 10, I'm hanging out on the beach, waiting for you to show up. Get your butt down here and don't forget your sunscreen.
T-bird

Good enough. I folded it in half and slipped it under her door, wondering exactly what time she'd eventually wake up and come find me. The beach called my name, and had been since I'd checked in, and it was time to make friends with the sand and surf.

The resort was much bigger on the ground level than it appeared from my balcony, and it took a fair bit of navigating to find the stairs I'd spotted that led to the beach. From my room, the light beige sand was deserted, and I understood why. Given the hidden entrance, no one would be able to find it, it was like a game of hide-and-seek. There were no signs to direct me. However, after passing by the adults-only pool, another pool with a swim-up bar, and another bar already lined with adults ready to start their vacation, I found the coveted stairs I'd spied from my room on the twenty-sixth floor and descended.

Palm leaves covered the narrow gap, leaving it cool

and breezy; no doubt a welcome reprieve from the heat for most tourists, but not me. It was -26°C when I left home yesterday, and the resort said today would hit +32°C. Bring it on. I could stand to lose the frostiness and thaw out.

My feet hit the beach and instantly a smile burst across my face. The powdery sand wrapped around my feet as I sank into its welcoming heat.

I walked, slowly and purposefully, over to a vacant lounge chair and dragged another to park beside me. This was where I'd planned on hanging out for the day. I tossed my bag of day essentials—sunscreen for my freckled, white Canadian skin, a couple of water bottles, my phone—I planned on making all my limited friends back home jealous with my Insta-worthy pics—and one of three novels I'd packed. The bag fell with a thud onto Camille's chair, and I draped my blue-and-white striped towel over the foot of my lounger.

Sunscreen rubbed in, floppy hat and sunglasses on, I sat cross-legged on the cushioned spot, taking in the million-dollar view and inhaling the relaxing and intoxicating scent of ocean air.

Bye-bye, city stress.

Hello, paradise.

Endless ocean stretched out ahead, the deep sapphire matching the imagined blue of my dreams.

Morning sunlight highlighted the island across the bay. Jet surfers hummed in the distance, cheers and screams punctuating the air as they bounced over the waves. A boat pulling a brave, or borderline crazy, parasailor slowed just enough to let their dangling feet touch the water. Yep, everyone in the vicinity was having a good time, living for adventure, and here I sat, taking it all in from the safety of my chaise lounge.

Yes, this was the life. For the next ten days, I was going to max out on my sunshine, get my vitamin D the natural way, and try my best to forget about my boring life back home. The co-workers who took great pleasure in throwing me under the bus. The kicked-out ex who could take his infidelity elsewhere. The new job with new people and new challenges. I shuddered. This trip was about finding myself, having a helluva good time, and connecting with Camille. A quick glance to my phone, which I promised to not be checking all the time, and it was almost ten. Where the hell was she?

You can sleep on the beach. Come join me. The view is to die for.

I stretched out my pasty-white legs, crossing them at the ankle, and snapped a pic of the sand, my toes and the waves. So cliché, but whatever. I'll retake the picture later in the week when I've gotten one of the spa pedicures and there's a decent start of a tan. That'll be fun.

Leaning back, I breathed in the salty air and allowed the rays of golden sunshine to warm me up and thaw me out, melting away all the frostiness inside as I closed my eyes. The waves gently rolled against the shoreline; the sounds so soothing it could've put me to sleep. Instead, I listened to the murmurs of the people behind me, the kids splashing in the pools, and the soft squishing of someone's feet in the sand.

For a breath it was just quiet. A perfectly welcome relief on my weary and mentally worn out self. A dark shadow covered me and not the kind that came with the clouds, as there hadn't been any. I sensed him before I dared open my eyes. With a sharp inhale of air, I stared at the pair of toned and sexy legs beside me, slowly allowing my gaze to roam upwards over a pair of dark swim shorts, up a white T-shirt, and setting on the tanned, handsome face taking me all in.

"T-bird, I presume?" There was a slight accent on the tip of his tongue, at once charming and intoxicating.

Oh crap. Had my note to Camille gone under the wrong door?

Chapter Two

The man in a plain white tee and blue board shorts pointed to the lounger beside me. "May I?"

"I'm saving that for someone."

He scanned the beach and smiled. It was an alluring smile, a little tipped on the one side and showcased a deep dimple on his left cheek. Appealing and downright sexy. "Fair enough."

His form was nice, like he worked out enough to take care of himself but not so much that he was egotistical about it and devoted all his waking hours to the gym. However, he sported more colour than me, had a head of dark wavy hair, and the start of a sexy five-o'clock shadow that started a few days back. The kind where guys don't care if they shave or not, yet somehow it still looks good. Wraparound shades prevented me from taking in his eyes. Damn. Those were the heart and soul.

A moment later, I blinked away my stares as he set

another chair beside me, a nice respectable distance away, yet still close enough to talk without yelling.

"So, T-bird," he said in a lilting accent I couldn't place. Not New York-ish, but close. "I'm going to be honest. I've never received a note like that."

"Well, that note was intended for someone else." I glanced around, craning my neck to see if it was a joke Camille was playing on me. Little Miss Sleepyhead was nowhere to be found. Where was she?

To the mystery note accepter, I raised my perfectly shaped eyebrow at him, thankful I had them done the day before I'd left. Everything had been waxed that morning. Everything. My lip, my underarms, my legs, and yes, I'd gotten an introduction to bikini waxing. Suffice it to say, I'll leave that alone and chalk it up to a what-was-I-thinking moment. Pretty sure the esthetician knew I wasn't coming back. "You've never received a note like that? Really?" Sarcasm rolled off my tongue. I didn't believe that at all.

"I had to come and check out who this T-bird was, and surprise, you are the only one on the beach."

Which was true. Unbelievably odd. "I know, isn't it crazy?" I sat up and crossed my legs like a yoga master. It was the most comfortable position to sit in. Maybe not the most ladylike, but I didn't care. "How are there so few people down here?"

The beach was almost ours alone, aside from a young couple making themselves at home in a cabana farther down the beach. I turned my gaze away. It was too early in the morning and a little too out in the open for that. I preferred my PDAs to be a little more refined and contained, and most definitely undercover.

"It gets busier towards the end of the day, when the heat wanes. By supper, there'll be no available seats."

"Well, that's good. Hate to think everyone comes here for the pool." Stay home if that's the case. I'd much rather be in the ocean, pushed around by waves. Even hearing the waves lap against the shoreline had a calming effect. "Been here long?"

"Got in two days ago."

So ... he wasn't from my area at all. WestJet from Edmonton only flew here on Saturdays and Wednesdays. "Where are you from?" I tried to penetrate the sunglasses and look into his eyes, imagining they were dark like his hair. Or maybe more exotic, like a mossy green. It would fit with his accent.

"Portland."

"Ah, I've been there when I was younger. We drove to Astoria and saw Mikey's house." Seeing the house from one of my favourite childhood movies was the highlight of that trip. Astoria had been one of the places we visited, but there had been others, just not as memorable. Oregon had been quite the drive from my hometown of Edmonton, but road trips were always fun with my family.

That grin of his widened. "Portland, *Maine*. Other side of the country."

What were people from Maine called? East Coasters? New Englanders? Not that it mattered. "Nice. I've never been there." Having lived in Edmonton all my life, of the limited places I've traveled, Maine was not on the list of places I'd seen. That was too far a drive.

"Where're you from?" He perched his feet on the lounger and dusted the sand from them. "No, wait, let me guess."

I kept my focus on the water, not wanting to give away any kind of clue. Camille said I was like an open book. However, sensing his gaze travelling up and down my body, I turned to make weak eye contact, pushing my own sunglasses up a bit to hide my eyes.

"Dark hair but pale skin. Hasn't seen true sunshine since the fall."

A smirk edged on my lips. "Wow. That narrows it down to a lot of places north of Mexico."

"True." He gave his whiskery chin a scratch. "You

have an accent though, so it's throwing me."

"I have an accent?" It was crazy enough that I started to laugh. I had zero accent. British people, they had accents. People from the deep South did too. I lived in Northern Canada. There were no accents there.

"Sure do. It's slight. Very ... Canadian."

Nice guess. I focused on him, hoping he couldn't see my gaze trailing over his strong jawline.

"Didn't you know Canadians have accents? You all sound different to us Americans. I worked in Toronto for a bit, and trust me, you all have an accent."

"And those from Maine don't?"

"Ah, maybe we do. I don't notice mine as much as I notice yours. However, I'm originally from Boston and those accents I recognize."

Well, that explained his entrancing accent; one I could easily listen to all day long. If he blabbed on about the stocks and bonds and weather, it would be music to my ears just listening to the way the words rolled off his tongue.

"By the way, I'm Jon." He extended his hand. "But you can call me lazybones if you prefer."

I shook his hand. Firm, but not too much so. "Jessica," I blurted out, momentarily ashamed for not revealing my real name. Whatever. It's not like I was going home with this guy. As soon as the playboy was done with me, he'd find another. Just as well. I'm not into one-night stands or short-lived romances. I wanted the satisfaction of falling so hard I couldn't imagine another living soul being so perfect. A dream to be sure, as it so rarely happens. Except to my parents.

"Jessica, it's a pleasure to meet you." He stretched out on his chair. "Mind if I stay a bit?"

"Not my beach." But I said it with a smile. I wasn't a bitch. Not always, anyway. I grabbed my phone, wondering where the hell Camille was. I sent her another text and a moment later, it pinged back.

Hey. Met someone late last night. Going to be a while.

When? I'd dropped her off at her hotel room late last night after we had a welcoming drink in the bar. *And what about Trey?*

Eh ... I need to think about him, but not now. I want to have fun. Take a note from my playbook. Live a little. Find yourself a guy or two or three. Go home satisfied and relaxed.

I threw a glance at the sexy guy beside me. Yeah, not an option. At least for me. Instead my gaze travelled to my bag where my book resided. That was more like it.

I typed back, *Can we at least meet up for supper?*

Already booked us reservations at Flora.

That was the Mexican a la carte restaurant on the resort. We were allowed to book there twice a week. The menu looked delicious, even if it was totally outside my level of comfort. *Great. When?*

Seven. L8R.

And that was the end of that. I was on my own until dinner. Sigh. I tucked my phone into the book I'd painstakingly cut a phone-sized hole in and set it on the edge of my chaise. No way would someone think to steal my copy of *Clan of the Cave Bear.*

"So, Jessica, tell me, what do you do for a living?"

A little forward, but nothing to set off warning bells. "I'm between jobs. Start a new one in two weeks."

"Doing?"

Dental hygiene sounded so boring. Who wants to know that I scrub teeth all day long? I loved it, and I loved that my patients left after a visit with clean and healthy teeth, but it's not a sexy job in the least. I could've lied and said anything. Instead, defeated, I told the truth before I could conjure up a more romantic-sounding job.

"That's cool."

I shrugged. "What about you?"

"I'm a web designer."

Whether he was telling the truth, I'd never know.

He could throw all sorts of web lingo at me to prove himself, and it could be believable.

"Sweet." Technology wasn't my strong suit. When I'd get an error message on my phone, I always called my brother first, who usually laughed and told me it was nothing to worry about.

"I'm my own boss, so it's a pretty sweet gig. I decide what jobs I want, and my timeline for working on them. If you ever need a website ..."

"I'll give you a call," I winked. He's probably not even named Jon. Not that he's given me any reason to not believe him. Still, he's a random stranger who took my note, assumed it was intended for him and came to find me. Weird.

"I'm getting hot. What about you? Want to go for a swim?"

Tess, the girl I was until I'd blurted out a false name, would've waited until this Jon vacated his spot, even if she was already feeling sun tinged. No way would she have stripped off her tank top and shorts in front of him, that's something Camille would've done, and probably had every guy drooling as she did it. It felt just a little too saucy for my liking. But then again, I was suddenly Jessica, and she was bolder and braver than me. "Sure." I pulled off my tank top and shimmied my shorts off, placing them over the top of my bag.

Jon had already removed his shirt revealing a taut, hairless chest. A tattoo in script ran along the inside of his bicep, and I was more than a little curious to know what it read.

Later. Maybe.

For now, it was time to play and have some fun.

"Race ya."

Chapter Three

I ran down the sand, feet digging in less and less as the water-soaked shoreline advanced. Jon was right behind me. Instead of touching the ocean like I wanted to, I sidestepped the waves and skirted over to the dock. My bare feet landed on the rough wood, and quickly, I raced down the vacant floating reprieve, past a dozen or so lounger chairs, and over to the far end. My toes stood poised on the edge, ready to launch me into the water, but I froze. I wanted to be sexy and make a perfect dive, but I didn't know how. And jumping in while holding my nose wasn't the epitome of elegance either.

Jon paused beside me. "Let's go."

I focused on the shoreline. We were quite the distance away, maybe two hundred feet, so the ocean floor should be far below. The resort owners would make sure it was safe, right? I found my feet again.

"Are you afraid?"

"Not at all." It wasn't fear that held me back. I studied the waves, seeing if there was anything I should worry about. Would they slam me against the dock? They didn't appear that strong, at least not here. The island further out in the ocean probably helped break up the strength of the waves.

Screw it. I am Jessica, wild and free. I plugged my nose and plunged into the ocean, feet first.

The moment they broke the surface, a chill shot through my body and as soon as I came up for air, I gasped. It wasn't as cold as I thought, but totally refreshing. It felt awesome.

Jon lowered himself in slowly, gripping the edge of the ladder. He tipped his head back into the water, and the ocean licked at the sides of his face. Righting himself, water ran out of his dark hair, spiraling down his neck. It was highly sexy. I brushed my own dark hair back figuring I looked more like a drowned rat than anything remotely attractive.

"Water's nice," I said. It wasn't the smartest words to roll out my mouth.

"Indeed."

The hum of a motor revved in the distance, and we both turned to watch. A parasailor floated behind the boat. Jon kept his focus on the half-naked man suspended under the parachute who had his arms extended a la Jack in *Titanic*. The words 'I'm the king of the world' almost sailed through the air. "I'm going to suck up the nerve to do that before I go home."

"Yeah, me too." But I knew it was shop talk. No way was I going to allow someone to drag me down a beach and hope everything worked well enough to yank me into the air. I had better ways of spending my money. Shopping for one. I was sure I passed a *mercado* on my way to the hotel.

The rivers of water were having all the fun washing down Jon's perfectly sculpted legs as he climbed back onto the dock.

I swam over to the ladder and pulled myself up, my own rivers running down my goose-pimpled skin. The contrast between the blazing sun and the cool ocean was heavenly. I stepped over to the edge of the dock and sat, dangling my feet in. "Well, I need a cool drink now. How about you?"

"Are you a good swimmer?"

I shrugged. "Decent enough. Couldn't save anyone's life though."

"Wanna race back to the shore? Last one there buys drinks."

My eyebrow shot up into my hairline. "The drinks

are free." It was a perk to staying at an all-inclusive.

"Fair enough. Then the first one there gets to select the drink."

I'm not a drinker by nature but I couldn't pass up the opportunity to show this guy who was boss. I may be a little rusty in my abilities, but it should come back like riding a bike, right? "Fine." I pushed myself off the dock and slipped into the water with a little less grace than I'd hoped. My suit caught and gave me an instant wedgie which I fixed under the cover of the water.

Jon remained on the dock.

"Aren't you coming in?"

"I prefer a little push. But to compensate, I'll give you a five-second head start."

I lined up next to the back of the dock, level to Jon. He'd be launching off at a weird angle, so my five-second advantage was going to pay off. "Whenever you're ready."

"Go," I said, my arms already cycling through the water. One. Two. Three. Four. Five. I didn't bother to see if he'd taken off yet, and I didn't hear a splash. Instead, I kept my focus on making sure my strokes were strong and smooth. I couldn't dive to save my soul, but I could swim. Eventually the bottom rose up to smack my hands, and I twisted to glance behind me to see where he was. There was no one in the ocean. How could he have passed me?

Yet sure enough, there he was in all his slicked-up glory standing by the chairs. How in the hell?

Salt water dripped off my body as I walked from the shoreline back to my undisturbed chair. Pleased that nothing had been touched or taken, I grabbed my towel and dried my hair off hoping the frizziness stayed away but knowing better. I finger brushed it into an unsecured braid and hoped for the best.

Footprints etched into the sand led to his chair and I followed their path to the water's edge. How did he do it? Coach Tremblay would've wanted a fast swimmer like him on the swim team, especially since I was useless and couldn't master a proper dive.

"It's killing you to know how I beat you, isn't it?"

"It's not killing me, but I am curious." Here I'd thought I was a decent swimmer, but not only had he beat me, he had time to walk up the beach to our spot. Impressive.

A resort worker crept by and Jon flagged him down. *"Dos cervezas, por favor."*

With a quick nod, the waiter disappeared.

Jon dug under his T-shirt and withdrew a fifty peso bill for a tip. To the worker it was probably big money. I'd noticed at breakfast how grateful they were for even ten pesos. Even with our paltry exchange rate, the fifty was the equivalent of $3.50, stupid cheap for a beer. It sucked how hard they all worked for so little. I vowed to be even more generous in my tipping.

The heat from the blazing sun pressed down on me, warming me up like an oven after I'd just exited the cool of the ocean.

I polished up my sunglasses, cleaning off the water spots and placed the wide-brimmed hat back on my head. Stretching out on the chair, I gave permission to the sun to dry my body off while at the same time sucking in my stomach and trying to look as flat as possible.

"Better reapply your sunscreen. You'll burn to a crisp."

"I think I'll be just fine." It was SPF 40 and waterproof at that.

He shook his head. "If you say so."

The waiter returned a few minutes later with beers so cold the outside of the bottle was ripe with condensation. Jon passed me one, and the chill felt so heavenly in my warm hands that I ran it over my chest for good measure, sighing as it created goose bumps in the process.

Jon held his bottle still in his hand and pointed the neck of it in my direction.

I tipped the bottle back and drank a few solid,

unladylike gulps and released a satisfying burp which I covered and hopefully stifled. "Damn, that hits the spot."

He laughed; a sweet and hardy sound. "I'll bet." Sand-crusted feet hit the edge of his lounger as he stretched out in his spot, remaining topless. The sun bounced rays off his perfect chest.

I tore my gaze away and let my eyelids softly shut, enjoying the peaceful sound of the waves, and in the far distance, the peals of children's laughter.

It was the sound of heavy feet and breathing that brought me to my senses. A large presence stopped beside my lounge chair and sent off a wave of paranoia that ignited my fine hairs to stand at attention.

"Dude, finally. You turn your phone off?" The voice was a tad panicked.

"I lost track of time. I was swimming and enjoying the presence of Jessica, here." Jon stood and in one fell swoop, pulled his white tee back over his delicious body. "Jessica, this is Irwin."

Not a name I would've given to the man beside my chair. He was more than intimidating with his distinct nod at being introduced. But it was totally weird that he was wearing black pants and a dark T-shirt. The man knew we were only a few degrees north of the equator, right? Who wears that much black in the tropics?

"Hey," he said in a higher pitched voice than I expected from a man of his size. "Bus leaves in ten minutes."

"Oh, shit. Do I have time to change?" He guzzled down the rest of his beer and shimmied the bottle into the sand.

"If you move your ass right now." Irwin's tone commanded more attention than his harsh words.

"Sorry, Jessica, I need to run. Can I meet up with you later?"

I smiled shyly. He was easy on the eyes and a resort-based crush and flirt would be harmless fun. "Sure." I stretched back out while Irwin tapped his watch. "If you can find me."

"Dude, we need to go."

Jon stood at the end of his chair and gave me a once-over. "Challenge accepted."

I listened as Jon and Irwin's chatter faded away and finished up my cool beer. *Challenge accepted.* I laughed. *What a guy.* After that, I closed my eyes and drifted to sleep. It was like being at home with the sound machine being on, except here the sunrays perfectly heated my body, unlike my electric blanket.

After a wee nap, I woke up. My hat had tipped

forward and therefore protected my face and part of my chest. However, I was now sporting a pink, wide-brimmed smile across the top of my breasts. Waterproof or not, a reapplication of sunscreen was vital here. My legs had been crossed at the ankle and thanks to the nap, they were two different colours: pink and white. Just great.

I had two choices. Take a quick dip in the ocean to cool off my skin or head back to my room and take an hour-long cold shower and apply some burn relief lotion, which I had the foresight to pack. The latter sounded better, so I gathered my things and took the two beer bottles and deposited them onto an empty serving tray.

The sun was incredibly hot. All around the bustling pool, the sun chairs were all shaded by giant umbrellas. I needed to remember that for tomorrow. There were no umbrellas on the beach, and that was likely the reason it was deserted in the heat of the day.

After a cool shower and another nap, I dressed in a white linen dress that showed off just how fast my Canadian skin can burn. It was time to meet Camille, so I headed to the main area of the resort where the à la carte restaurants were. This resort had five, which was almost unheard of. I didn't need to eat at the sprawling buffet for every meal of the day, just the first two, and based on how I'd dined this morning, maybe only one. The à la cartes were all themed: Mexican, Italian, Japanese, Indian and a seafood speciality. I wasn't sure where that one was, though, but the tour guide on the bus mentioned it was on a boardwalk along the beach. However, I didn't remember seeing any restaurant when I was down there.

I hung around the entrance to the à la carte. All of them, aside from the seafood experience, entered through the same main door before branching off. A few minutes after I checked on our reservation, Camille emerged from the elevator in all her magnificent glory, a slinky grey dress showing off her toned body. Her blonde hair was piled on her head, and as always, she was stunning. Sometimes I wondered if I had a girl-crush on her as even her outer beauty rivaled her inner beauty.

"Hey, sunshine," Camille said as she got closer. "Look who got some colour today." She ran her fingers over the edge of my burn and made a sizzling sound. "Ouch."

"Yeah. I spent some time on the beach. What were you up to today?"

"Let's sit, and I'll tell you." She linked her arm through mine and led me over to the hostess.

We checked in and were escorted to a table with a seaside view. A bonus was watching the sunset, and judging by the magnificent colouring in the sky, we were in for a spectacular show.

"So?" I placed the cloth napkin over my lap. "Who is he, and how did you meet?"

"Well, last night after our Welcome to Mexico drinks, I came back down. I just wasn't tired. They had the music going, and I made myself at home. This one guy, Wade, yeah, that's his name." Her head bobbed in recall. "Anyway, he and I hit it off and danced until they shut the place down. Like, around two or something. I was pretty hammered, and so was he. I asked him if he wanted to continue the party up in my room, and we grabbed a few drinks to take upstairs." She winked at me. "I think I wore more of the drink, if you catch my drift. Word to the wise, ice on the body is tantalizing." Her eyebrows danced. "It was the most fun experience I've had in a long while."

"You dawg." I playfully swatted her hand.

"Good thing they change the sheets. My bed was … a little sticky." She didn't even blush.

"And Trey?" They'd been together for months.

She shrugged and took a sip of her water. "Whatever. He thinks it's okay to sleep around. Two can play his game, he can consider it revenge. Besides, these guys don't live in butt-fuck Alberta, and I'm never going to see them again. They're not even Canadian. Well, not all." She jutted her nose out. "Except maybe him. Ghosts have more colour." A peaceful sound breathed out of her and she draped a napkin over her lap. "You know, I could live here. Couldn't be too hard to find a job on the resort." She waved her hand, and I understood. It was hard to hate on a place as beautiful as the tropics where it never snowed, the heat was welcome and the sun shone all the time.

"What did you do all day today with this Wade guy?"

With Camille, there was no holding back. "We fucked. Endlessly. It was ah-mazing. Trey's a one timer, then he's done. But Wade … Wow. Over and over again. His stamina. Incredible. A girl could get used to that." She ran her hands over the top of her breasts and a contented sigh breathed out of her. "Ever had sex in a shower?"

I cleared my throat as the waiter arrived. We ordered shots of tequila to get our evening started and an appetizer.

"Are you going to see him again?"

"Maybe." She scanned the terrace. "He's not the only guy here though. There are lots of hot guys. Who knew revenge sex was so wild?"

I checked out the other guests. Yeah, hot guys were definitely in abundance. There had to be one at every table. And the majority of them were in our age range, late twenties to early thirties. But, a lot of them were also sitting with pretty women so it did lessen the playing field.

Camille nudged me. "What about you? What were you up to all day?"

"I wasn't working up a sweat, if that's what you mean. At least, not with someone else. I hung out on the beach, went for a swim in the ocean." With a gorgeous guy. For a little while at least. Speaking of which … "What's your room number again?"

"2432. Why?"

Damn. I was off by one number. The note should've slid under the door beside Jon's. Oh well. "Just wondering. I was going to come by and knock this morning, but I couldn't remember if you were thirty-two or thirty-one."

"The room next door has a hot guy in there." She fanned herself. "I should make myself known to him."

A part of me knew if she threw herself at him, he'd been lured into her charms and the little tentacles of a jealous nature wrapped around me. Not that I had a chance with him anyway. He was just some guy I had a beer with on one of the most beautiful beaches in the world, who accepted a weak challenge to find me later. As cute as he was, I couldn't see myself bedding him. Well, I could actually. If we were in an adult relationship and had known each other for a few months first. But after one meeting? Never. And certainly not within the week I was here. That was a Camille thing, not a Tess thing.

"Hey, welcome back." Camille smiled. "You took off on me for a sec. Drinks here." She lifted her shot and clanked it against mine. "Bottoms up, girlfriend." She winked and tipped the amber-coloured fluid back.

I followed suit and downed my shot, ending with a shudder. I wasn't a fan of tequila. "Wow."

I opened the leather-bound menu and perused the few choices for dinner. Each meal came with an appetizer, a salad, a dinner of choice, and followed with a dessert. No wonder they recommended booking a couple of hours. It would be an experience for sure.

Deciding what I wanted to eat, preferably something tame and known, I set my menu down. "I was flipping through the hotel guide and there are lots of neat things to do while we're here. I'd love to go whale watching and do the turtle release." Both of those sounded pretty tame. There were other, more adrenaline-based excursions, but not to my liking.

She didn't move her focus off the menu. "Nah. I'm content to hang out on the resort and relax."

"I'd pay for your outings." Camille had drained her meager savings to join me. She'd never been a penny-pincher or a saver, rather a-spend-as-you-get-it type person. Actually, I was pretty sure she lived off her credit card. I, on the other hand, always had been a saver. My savings were very well padded, so much so, that taking time off between jobs *and* throwing in a ten-day trip barely scraped the surface.

Peeling her gaze off the nice selection of food choices, she gave me a look that suggested I end that conversation instantly.

"So," I said, changing the topic back to our relaxing plans. "Want to hang out on the beach or the pool tomorrow?"

"If it's the pool, one of us needs to get there early and save seats. Wade says after eight there's nothing available."

That wasn't that early, at least for me. "Sure, I'll grab the seats. It'll be fun to hang out by the infinity pool all day and swim up to the bar."

"Great, can you get seats in the adults only pool? I don't want to be splashed by the kids."

I sighed. The adults only pool was surrounded by bushes and trees, closing it off. There was no beach view from that area. It was something I couldn't wrap my head around. Why would you come here and not take in the view? "Are you sure? The beach view is pretty amazing."

I looked out west to drive my point home.

The sun was nearing the horizon, sending golden rays of oranges and pinks across the sky. It didn't even hurt to stare at the orb as it lowered itself, eventually touching the edge of the ocean. It was beautiful.

"Yeah, I'm sure. Besides, if we party tonight, you're not going to want to listen to the screams of children either." She gave me a soft nod. "That's why these restaurants are nicer than the buffet one. No kids here." She sighed and shifted in her seat. "I deal with those little brats all day long so don't take it so personally that I want a break from them. It doesn't make me a bad person."

"I never said that."

"No, but your face did." She pointed at me. "Here, I'm not Miss Evans. Here, I'm Camille, the Canadian partygoer. You should crawl out of your shell a bit too. Ditch the girl you are at home and unleash your inner goddess. Because honestly, you're a fucking knockout, and there could be a hell of a party between your legs if you'd let it happen."

"Thanks, Camille." I wasn't sure if it was a back-handed compliment or not. Who was I back home? A dedicated employee. I was, until I had to quit. My co-workers were making my life hell and reporting their behaviour to the boss only made the situation worse. Boss was probably as bad as they were, anyway. Just as well I got out. The new dental office seems much more professional. Time to move on to bigger and better things.

Mesmerized, I watched as the sun fully immersed itself in the ocean, turning off its full glow. All around us, a flickering of soft lights lit up the terrace, and the waiter appeared out of nowhere and ignited the candle in the center of our table.

"Another round of drinks, please," Camille asked him and watched as he walked away. "You know, I could get used to this. It's so much nicer than back home." She placed her hand on mine and squeezed. "Thanks for asking me to join you. I love that you are my best friend and that you asked me to get away with you and help you unwind."

"I love you too."

"Maybe here, you'll even find your happiness again." Stretching out her other hand, she tucked some of my hair behind my ear.

Camille always got extra affectionate with alcohol, which is probably how she convinced Wade to join her own personal party. I didn't worry. Camille was a control freak and was able to defend herself in just about any situation. To me, her affection was just Camille being Camille, and the constant touching she did never bothered me. Jumping her chair closer to mine, she caressed my cheek and leaned against my shoulder.

The weight of a thousand stares pulled me away from the top of Camille's head as I searched the terrace for the source. Suddenly I made eye contact with Jon.

Challenge completed.

Chapter Four

Camille had another couple of rounds and drank mine as well. The drinks were stronger in the a la carte restaurant than they were on the pool deck, and it hit Camille pretty hard. Her inhibitions were no longer inhibited. She rubbed my thigh. Or my back. Or she twirled my hair. I didn't mind because it was Camille, my best friend since grade school. What bothered me were the stares and sly smiles I'd catch on Jon's face when I made eye contact. How lucky that he was sitting two tables over and had a direct line of sight to my drunk and flirtatious best friend, who strangers would probably think was my overzealous lover.

The meal was finished, and I left a hefty tip for the waiter tucked under my water glass. Camille had flirted incessantly with him and he looked very uncomfortable. Even I was borderline annoyed, and I was used to it. The huge tip was my apology for allowing her to continue drinking as I should've stopped her at least a round ago. Probably two rounds if I was being honest.

"Alrighty, time to go." I braced myself and gave my hand to Camille to pull her to a stand.

She was a dead weight and yanked so hard I thought my arm would break free from its socket. "You're so beautiful, Tess." She ran her hand down the side of my cheek.

Heat flooded across my face. "And you're so drunk."

"Nope. I feel fine."

As much as I wanted to believe that, I knew better. Her first step was a stumble, and I nearly missed catching and righting her. It was going to be a long walk back up to the hotel room.

"Do you need a hand?" Jon rose as I pulled Camille passed his table.

"She just needs to walk it off, but thanks."

"I love you, T-bird." Camille tipped her head onto my shoulder and wrapped her arm around my waist.

I somehow managed to stagger Camille out into the lobby and up to her hotel room, an adventure which took a full thirty minutes. The resort wasn't that big, she was just that drunk and everything was suddenly very interesting. Ever watched a drunk person have a conversation with a pot of flowers? Not nearly as amusing as it sounds. And when her reflection in the elevator talked back, the squeal that exited her rivaled a child's at seeing Santa Claus.

Even digging her key card out was a battle, but I finally found it and unlocked her room.

"Ah, home," she said, freeing her feet from her sandals, which slid across the room. She flopped over to the bed, ignoring the swan made out of towels, and fell face first into the white duvet. "Just let me sleep for a little bit, and then we can go out. Go dancing in the bar or go to the games room."

She was a lightweight with her alcohol. Almost like she had a borderline intolerance of it. It didn't take much for it to affect her and tonight proved that. With all the food, the five or six shots should not have knocked her out. She should've paced herself more but really, as her best friend, I should've intervened.

I put her phone and key card on the desk and sat beside her, rubbing her back. "Oh, Camille. What am I going to do with you?" Grabbing the remote, I flipped on the TV, however, everything was in Spanish, and I was in no mood to translate it all inside my head. It was a process as I translated into French, which I knew well and then into English. Tonight, I didn't have the energy. Instead, I stretched out beside Camille and closed my eyes.

After a few blissful moments of solitude, Camille bolted upright and covered her mouth. "Time to go, Tess." She ran for the bathroom.

Another good thing about Camille was she knew my limitations and being around someone while they were physically ill was one of them. Before her retching sounds assaulted my ears, I was already out the door. Just knowing she was throwing up was enough to turn my stomach and make me feel ill, I'd likely be joining her prayers to the porcelain god if I didn't escape. Camille had once told me I was a physical empath, whatever the hell that meant. I thought it was more like I just couldn't stand the sound of barfing.

I made sure the door was closed and locked and headed over to the elevator. It was still early and going back to my own room wasn't an appealing thought when there was still so much to see and do. Upon stepping into the elevator, I spotted a sign for the nightly entertainment. Tonight's performance was the Mexican take on *Grease*. Having memorized the movie from watching it a hundred times as a kid, it sounded like a fun way to pass the time.

It was a nice walk over to the other part of the resort where the play was about to be performed. The theater area was tucked behind the resort, impossible to have seen from my balcony, which was surprising given the size of the place. A stage sat at the far end and there had to be over two hundred chairs set up. I picked one near the front and off to the side.

"Can't wait to see who plays Kenickie."

I turned in the direction of the male voice, wondering if he'd been addressing me.

Jon sat in the chair behind me, smiling his charming dimpled smile. "Good evening, Jess." He winked at me, and for a moment I had the chance to take in his soulful eyes. They weren't dark like I'd thought or a mossy green. Instead, under the stage lights, they were a soft blue, almost grey.

Right, I was Jessica. "Good evening." I returned my focus to the stage. A cardboard cutout of Greased Lightning sat propped up on the left side, near the stairs.

"Where's your date?"

"My best friend," I corrected, "is up in her room puking." I hung my head, shame filling me as I just absolutely can't handle being around a sick person. Had I been paying more attention to her, I would've stopped the drinking from getting out of hand.

"Yuck."

"I agree. That's why I'm here. I'm a terrible human for not being compassionate about that, or worse, not even being able to physically stomach helping her. But I'll check on her in a bit." I waved my phone. "She'll text me when the worst is over."

"I don't think that knocks on your compassion. I think it means you know your limits."

"Anyway ..." I turned my attention back to him and searched out his entourage, that big guy Irwin and the petite lady who ate supper with them. "Where are your friends?"

"This kind of thing doesn't interest them in the least." He rose and pointed to the chair beside me. "May I move there?"

"Sure."

"Great, it's a little awkward talking to the side of your face, as beautiful as it is."

Well damn. That was the sweetest thing I've been told in a long while. He inched in front of me, and I took every opportunity to check out the perfect ass moving beneath a pair of white pants. They fit him like a glove—not too tight and not so baggy it was all left to the imagination. There was enough showcased to send my imagination sailing.

"That's better," he said, sitting and readjusting the chair. He crossed his legs and placed his hands in his lap.

I pulled my wrap over my shoulders as a warm breeze blew through the area. "So, how was your dinner?"

"Amazing. The food is so good. How's yours?"

"Great. My friend is a little cautious with her eating, but she managed to find something to enjoy. I liked the variety to choose from and had the goat meat tacos with extra hot sauce."

"Yeah, I like things spicy too." He winked and I cast my gaze to the ground.

Spicy would not be a category I fell into. Fact was, Camille was the adventurous one who had the goat meat tacos while I ate the more cautious foods, such as the enchiladas with ground beef and a mild sauce. But whatever, I wasn't dining with Jon.

"Tomorrow ... do you have plans?"

"Oh yeah, big plans." That beach was calling my name, however, this time I'd be more proactive in my sunscreen application.

"Ah, too bad. I'm taking a sailing tour over to the island tomorrow. Rumor has it, on the west side, there is a nudist beach, and there's supposed to be an authentic eatery. Everything's cooked over a fire since there's no electricity. Thought maybe you'd want to join me."

"On the nudist beach?" I scoffed. Dream on, lover boy.

He shook his head. "Oh, God, no. Not my thing. I wouldn't mind collecting a few starfish to take home.

They're supposed to be plentiful over there as long as the naked tourists are gone."

"You know it's illegal, and that they kill those, right? The ones you buy in the *mercados?* They haven't died of natural causes."

"Really?"

"So I've heard." I shrugged, not remembering who had told me that. But it stopped me from ever buying one.

The opening lyrics of *Grease* blasted through the speakers, crackling in intensity and silencing any further conversation. Although the show was magnificent with the actors singing and dancing and generally doing a bang-up job, I couldn't keep my focus on them entirely. Jon kept checking me out and moving in his seat, attempting to drape his arm on the back of my chair. He didn't get that far, but it wasn't for a lack of effort. I'd like to think it was because he was nervous or something.

Forty minutes later they wrapped up with a huge finale, running into the audience and pulling people onto their feet. I was one, and at first, I wanted to say no and firmly glue my ass to the chair, but jumping up and dancing like no one cared, that was something *Jessica* would do. Besides, no one here knew I was a terrible dancer, and most likely, they probably didn't care either.

I hopped up and joined the guy who played Sonny

and did my best imitation of the hand jive. It was more like some kind of fit as I nearly hit him in the face, but still it was fun. There was something oddly freeing about laughing and having a hoot in front of complete strangers. I wished Camille could've seen it.

The song ended as the lights on the stage dimmed and the rest of the area lit up. Party was over.

"You were great." Jon appeared by my side.

"You should've come up. Frenchie did ask you to dance."

"No thanks. I prefer to sit and watch."

"Do you now?" It came out before I could stop myself.

He responded by smirking. "Come on, I'll walk you back to the main part of the resort." He offered me his arm, which I hesitated to take. "I promise I don't bite."

Slowly, I wrapped my fingers around his arm, and watched his face attempt to hide his delight. I hoped I was more successful in keeping mine under wraps.

"Shall we?" He led me out of the courtyard.

We roamed silently along a lit path back to the main entrance of the resort. The breeze was warm as it blew around us. Gentle sounds from wind chimes joined the rhythmic chirping of the grasshoppers. It was a beautiful symphony and a feast for the ears. I could've stayed out on the path for the whole evening, but alas, I followed Jon into the lobby.

"Care to grab a drink?" He released my hand.

"On one condition."

"And that would be?"

"We take it outside. It's too nice to be inside." And it was quieter. Even through the glass doors the music blared. I wasn't in a party mood; I'd rather enjoyed the cozy, borderline romantic walk back and didn't want the night to end.

"Fair enough." He held open the door.

The bass was an assault on my eardrums and soul. We marched through crowds of people, both young and old, as we passed two pool tables and several bar-height tables littered with glasses filled with a multitude of coloured fluids.

At the bar, Jon leaned against the wooden railing. "What would you like?" He cupped his hand around my ear, his warm breath tingling against it as he tried to not yell over the music.

"A cabana." Yes, I preferred the froufrou girly drinks, and the cabanas were right up my alley. Pina colada mix, vodka, and grenadine to give it a healthy pink flush. I wasn't much of a beer drinker, nor a straight up hard liquor consumer. I needed the sweet.

He gave me a look that questioned my sanity, but turned to the bartender. *"Dos cabanas, por favor."*

Drinks in hand, he motioned back to the lobby, which I happily led us to, holding the door open for him this time. Once the doors closed, the volume dropped by seventy-five percent and we were free to talk at a normal level.

He handed me a pink drink. "Your cabana."

"Cheers." I clinked it against his and walked over to the stairs, descending the tiled steps to the main floor. A few feet away from the stairwell, the open air greeted me like an old friend, and I welcomed the embrace.

I decided against the tables scattered around the pool and instead parked my butt on a rattan couch built for two, it felt a little more romantic sharing the seat. Jon sat beside me, and we were close enough that our knees touched.

We were in a darker part of the resort, but not in total darkness. Lights from the nearby pools provided ambient lighting, as did the inset lights around the paths. Where the daytime was prone to more of a boisterous atmosphere, the evening was soft and romantic.

"It's beautiful here."

"It is." He starred straight into my soul.

A resort employee shuffled by us, making eye

contact with me. *"Buenas noches."*

"Buenas noches," I replied, speaking it perfectly with the right inflections.

Jon waited until we were alone. "Have you checked out the full resort?"

"Mostly. Have you?" I asked smugly.

"Yep. Last couple of nights I've sat on the boardwalk and listened to the waves and stared up at the stars."

"The boardwalk?" I took a sip of my pink drink, letting the coolness devour the flames inside.

"You haven't checked it out? It's right on the beach. It's a mile-long connection between us and the resort next door. Closer to their side, there's this amazing seafood restaurant. Do you love crab and oysters?"

To be honest, I hate all forms of seafood. Camille calls me a child for my food choices. "Who doesn't?" I downed the rest of my drink, not surprised by the ease with which it disappeared.

"Want to check it out? I could show you the stars along the way."

No.

Yes.

No. It could all be a trap, and he'd be leading me to my death by luring me away from the roving staff and odd security person. I knew the safety record was very high, it's one of the reasons I chose this resort, but still … However, he did walk me safely back from the theatre without incident.

I checked out the man beside me, who awaited my answer. Patiently and without prodding, he sat there with his long legs crossed and his arm resting along the back of the couch. Instantly, I stood, throwing Tess's caution to the wind and channeling my inner Jessica, who'd better not be getting me into trouble. "Take me to the boardwalk and show me the stars."

Chapter Five

We descended a set of stairs that led to the infinity pool and then another set that took us to the beach. Those stairs I was familiar with, and when we got to the sand, I pulled off my strappy heels and carried them, reveling in the cool sand squishing between my toes.

"This way." Barefoot, he led me past the beach chairs all piled up against the edge of a wall, which I hadn't really paid much attention to earlier today. A deck-like surface was all lit up in a white glow that came from the bottom of the railing. The boardwalk. No wonder he'd seemed surprised that I hadn't noticed it. Idiot.

A stairwell sat in the sand, and he stopped at the edge. "Put your shoes on before you climb. There's a lot of bird shit up here."

So much for a romantic, barefoot stroll. Although, the hundred-foot walk through the damp sand was nice. I stepped up to the first stair free of sand and dusted my feet off before securing my shoes. Jon followed, slipped back into his loafers, and set his empty glass on the banister.

He reacted to the confused look on my face. "They come and collect them. Trust me."

"Okay. It just seems silly to leave your glass behind."

"There's nowhere to put it."

Fine, but I couldn't do it. I'd rather wait and drop it off than leave it sitting like litter. I walked ahead of him, the heels of my shoes clacking on the wooden boardwalk. Following it around a slight bend, the tower of the resort disappeared behind the foliage and greenery of the jungle-like garden that sat on the edge of the beach.

It was just Jon, myself, the ocean lapping against the posts, and an endless sea of twinkling stars. We roamed a little further around to an alcove that jutted out from the main boardwalk. A little pier, all lined with the same under-railing lights.

"Here," Jon said, his voice sparking with excitement. "This is the place. But this corner is the best."

I stepped over to the recommended corner and gazed out. If I leaned over enough, the million stars twinkled a little brighter in the inky sky, and the waves splashing against a pile of rocks were a little louder. The crests of each wave glowed under the LED lighting. It was a magical view that left me breathless.

"I see why you come here." My words were barely audible, for fear any sound louder than a whisper would ruin the majesty of the moment.

"Yeah, it's very peaceful." He leaned on the railing and looked over at me. "There seems to be a lot of clarity that comes with staring out into the darkness."

I chuckled. "Stargazer, are you?"

"Full-time, but only in my former life."

"Oh yeah, when was that?" I expected him to say the early 1900s or something. Some people truly believed in reincarnation.

"Three years ago." His face hardened briefly, and his hands twisted together.

Not the answer I anticipated. "You don't have to say any more. Some things are better left unsaid." I turned and leaned my back against the wooden railing.

"It's okay." He gave his earlobe a rub.

Hearing someone's sob story, which I suspected I was about to hear, always killed a small part of me and left me reeling in their pain. Part of that whole empath thing, I supposed. I sensed a sadness in him, but maybe him releasing it out into the open breeze would help it float away. I moved to the other side of him so I could be upwind but tried to disguise it as interest in the rocks below. "So? What happened? Girl troubles?"

"That would make things easier, wouldn't it?"

I shrugged not knowing.

"It was a myriad of things. The most important being that three years ago I was given a diagnosis that would change my life; I'm slowly going blind, and my vision is tunneling." There was no fear in his voice, no sadness, just a matter of fact tone. It blindsided me with its humility. He extended his hands out in front of him and made a circle, like a child would of a pretend scope. "My field of view used to be this." The tips of his fingers and thumbs touched. "Now, it's more like this." The first two knuckles on his right hand slid under the left. It was a significant difference.

I held my breath.

"I have a couple years left until I get total darkness, so I'm trying to see everything and do everything that requires sight, because when it's gone, I'll never be able to view it again." His hands fell back to the railing and he held tight as he leaned back.

"Wow." *What was the right thing to say to that? I'm sorry? That sounded so cliché, even though I was sorry it was happening to him.* "It must've been hard to hear that diagnosis." He gave me a peculiar look, one that I took to heart. Dumb things were always known to fall out of my mouth, usually at the worst of times. I shook my head. "I'm sorry, I don't know how to respond to that without seeming blasé about it. It's really an awful thing to hear."

"Thank you for being honest about that." He gazed out across the sea. "I've received a lot of apologies over the last couple of years, but that's expected, I guess. It's refreshing to hear something other than that." He leaned back, pulling on the railing and after a heartbeat righted himself again. "Truth be told, I didn't know how to respond either when I was first diagnosed. To say I was gobsmacked would be an understatement."

"Gobsmacked? That's a word I haven't heard in a long while." A small smile etched on his face. Had he said that to lighten the mood? "I can't even imagine what that moment was like, but devastating would probably be a good descriptor." To hear that your world would be given a giant shift and something you took for granted would be taken away from you would be terrible news to digest. It would take me a long time to accept that.

"Completely true. I had to assess a lot of issues in my life, figure out what's important, and make up a bucket list of things I wanted to do and places I wanted to see."

A star high in the heavens flickered a reddish wink. "What's on your list of things to see and do while here?"

"Everything?" He laughed and connected with me.

"I'm taking the water taxi out in the afternoon, as the sunset sail was booked. Later in the week, I'm going on a quad tour through a coffee and coconut plantation, and zip-lining through the jungle. It would be sweet to spot a monkey or something. And I'm trying to book an excursion to go snorkeling as well, but I have a teensy fear of deep water, so I'm not sure if I'll go."

"But you swam back with me today."

"No, I raced you."

I tipped my head.

"You swam. I ran the length of the dock."

Duh, of course. "So that's how you beat me. I'd been wondering." I brushed a few stray strands of hair away from my face and allowed my gaze to linger over his apologetic face.

"I cheated. I'm sorry." He hung his head.

"You ordered the beers afterwards, and tipped the server. Apology accepted." I gave him a smile and squeezed his arm.

"What about you? What's your story?"

I shrugged and turned away from him, facing out to the bay. "I have no story."

"Everybody has a story."

"Yeah. Well, mine's closed and locked up tight. I'd rather not revisit it." The way he stared into me was unnerving, as if his gaze lingered long enough, he'd pierce through the depths of my soul and unlock the mysteries. Not tonight. Not ever. My gaze roved over where I imagined the horizon ended and the inky twinkles of the night sky began. "What constellations do you know?"

"All of them."

"What? Really?" Science class was boring to me; it brought my average down. Still, it taught me how to memorize, as recalling basic facts was key to passing.

"Yes. I am a part-time astronomer. Back home I work at our local observatory, but my time is limited. However, I've studied the stars forever."

"I only know the W." As if he needed me to point it out, but I did anyway.

"Ah, Cassiopeia. The Queen of Ethiopia." He turned his handsome face up towards the flickering lights. "She was vain and figured her beauty was far superior than that of the sea nymphs. Cassiopeia strongly believed her daughter, Andromeda, was also of a beauty beyond that of the Nereids, the nymph daughters of the sea god Nereus, who often was seen in the presence of Poseidon."

"Andromeda's the galaxy, right?"

"It's named after her." He stood beside me and wrapped an arm around me, pointing his hand out skyward. "Andromeda, the galaxy, sits about there. That fuzzy little disc."

I followed the length of his strong, muscular arm, over his hand, and to the tip of his pointer finger. Searching the area around his bitten nail tip, I finally spotted what I thought was a fuzzy little disc.

"But the story turns dark. Cassiopeia and her husband, King Cepheus—which is that house constellation there." He slowly pointed out a childlike drawing of a house on the other side of the W. The roof was at an awkward angle and the sides of the house drew inwards, if I went based on the five major points of light. "They had to sacrifice Andromeda, as Cassiopeia had angered the gods."

"Why?"

"To punish the Queen for her arrogance, Poseidon sent a sea monster after her kingdom. King Cepheus consulted with the oracle and found the only way to stop the ravaging of their kingdom was to sacrifice their daughter."

"And he did?"

"Chained her to a rock where she waited for the whale or sea monster to take her away."

I gasped. "That's terrible. Is there a whale constellation above Andromeda that looks like it's eating her, or is the whale all around her like that bible story?"

"That's Jonah. Very different mythology. However, there is a constellation near Andromeda of the whale." His face was close enough that I felt the bulging of his cheeks as they pressed into mine. "Cetus is right there." He drew an invisible line connecting the dots of what he claimed was a whale.

There were no stars in any pattern that I recognized as being part of a whale. That was a huge stretch. Still, the story had me intrigued.

"But her story doesn't end there."

I continued to stare at the stars, loving the tale he told. I never knew there was anything more than random stars in some weird configurations, and here he was spinning a magical love story of beauty and arrogance and sacrifice.

"Andromeda was rescued by her hero, Perseus. He was just returning home from having slain Medusa, and when he saw the sea monster near Andromeda, he held up Medusa's head and turned that whale into stone, which dissolved in the ocean. Perseus set her free and married her. So … in the night sky, he's always beside her. Just as her mother sits above her and the King beside the Queen."

"Wow." I was breathless and devoid of words of a higher caliber.

"There are so many stories woven into the heavens.

That's my favourite one though because most people know Cassiopeia and have at least heard of Andromeda."

Yep, I fell into that category as I knew those two names. However, now I had a story to share with my friends the next time I looked up to the stars.

"Fun fact. In November, there is a meteor shower that radiates out of Perseus. It's one of the best shows of the year. And sometimes the weather is perfect for cuddling up on an air mattress and watching the streaks of light zip across the sky."

"I've never watched."

"Book your calendar. You need to watch it at least once in your life. It's incredible to see." He trailed off on the last word.

To see.

How much was Jon trying to commit to memory? The thought of trying to see everything pained me. I couldn't even imagine. All the little things we took for granted, and he was trying to capture them like a photograph to store in his mind forever.

"I can't wait to watch in November." And it was a promise I intended to keep. I twisted my head to take him all in. His eyes melted into mine, and his hand found mine resting on the railing. My fingertips had heated up as my core churned to life. I wanted to kiss this man, this person who just this morning was a complete stranger. I wanted to be the wild and reckless one, like Camille, and as I channeled her into my thoughts, Jon broke away.

"Do you want to walk to the Oyster Bar and grab a light snack?"

I wasn't hungry, at least not for food, but I wasn't ready to call it a night with Jon either. Hand in hand, I followed him down the boardwalk.

Chapter Six

Standing in front of the excursions board at the front desk the next morning, I stared at limited options though I was as sure as the sun shines that there were more than this. Three options only, and the one I was most interested in—the sunset sail—had a Sold Out sign pinned overtop. Something deep inside me told me I needed to get Jon on that, and it would be sweet if I could join him, plus he'd mentioned how he tried and could only get the afternoon version. I wanted him to experience, *to see*, an ocean sunset. The one last night from the terrace of the Flora was pretty damn magnificent. It had to be even better off shore.

"Uh, excuse me," I said in my most perfect high school Spanish, which is to say it was craptastic. "I'm wondering if you have any availability for tonight's sunset sail."

"Senorita, all full." He pointed to the sign with a

look I could only sum up as annoyed.

"I know that." I leaned forward so the people lingering nearby couldn't hear. Making a spectacle, which I was prepared to do if I absolutely needed to, wasn't high on my to-do list. "My friend just informed me that he's going blind." I hoped I used the right words in Spanish, "And he's desperate to see the sunset. How can I make this happen for him? Whatever it costs. *Por favor.*" I'd dip into my savings if need be. That's what credit cards were for. For good measure, I pulled it out and set it on the desk.

He clicked on the keyboard rapidly. A pause, where he took me in and the pitiful sad expression I was giving and resumed clicking. He did this off and on before picking up the phone and rapidly speaking Spanish to whoever was on the other end. He spoke way too fast for me to understand but I did catch a couple of words like urgent and tonight.

I searched around the open-air lobby, my gaze landing on Camille who sat on a nearby wicker chair. She was still a little green from last night and only woke up a few minutes ago.

He set the phone into the cradle and typed on the keyboard. "Senorita, you in luck." An ancient dot matrix printer hummed behind him, and he tore off the printout with paper tracks. "Captain says there's room for two more." On the paper were two barcodes. He handed me the tickets.

Without hesitation, I passed him my credit card.

"No. No charge." He pushed the credit card back in my direction, eyes darting everywhere. "Be here at five. Shuttle to the dock leaves at five fifteen. You board at five thirty. Bring a jacket. It gets chilly."

"Gracias, senor." I pulled a fifty peso note from my wallet, grateful for his willingness to get me on tonight's sail. *"Por favor."* I tucked the edge of it under his keyboard, and I folded the tickets and practically skipped over to Camille.

She rose and smoothed out the short skirt she wore over her swimsuit. "Did you get them?"

I flashed the papers at her. "No charge, either."

"Of course not. That excursion is free. Didn't you read that? The ones booked through the resort are *gratis.*" Camille laughed and instantly I felt like a dumbass. Still, it was sold out and somehow, I got two tickets. "However, you book through them ..." She pointed to the airline we'd booked our all-inclusive through. "And it's, how do you say? *Mucho dinero?*"

I walked over to meander the airline's offerings, having glossed over that spiel on the flight. They offered so many off-site excursions. Whale watching, although it was off-season by a month, ATV rides, zip-lining, snorkeling and more. Everything read like a bit of an adrenaline buzz. "These all sound like the things Jon mentioned doing."

"Easy there, T-bird. Just because a guy mentions something he wants to do, doesn't mean you have to buy it for him."

I mocked shock, as if I would. "Hey. I'm not buying it for him, I'm just checking it out. In case I want to join in."

Camille started choking on her own spit and thumped her hand against her chest. "I'm sorry, did my best friend just say she wanted to go zip-lining?" She pointed to the picture of a person strapped into a contraption, dangling precariously over the top of a jungle. "Who is this guy?"

"I'm not doing it because of a guy." There, I said it. It wasn't like I was going to go. A fear of heights would stop anyone from even considering zip-lining.

"Sure you are. But whatevs, I'm starving. Let's eat. Beside you need to find lover boy and give him his ticket."

"He's not my lover boy." We didn't even kiss. It was there between us, I'm sure. So many opportunities and he turned away whenever the moment felt right. Or when it felt right to me at least. Maybe he didn't feel the same.

But if he didn't, why did we get an available table at the oyster bar and dine on yucky clams? I even pounded back some heavy-duty *cafe de olla*? Something was there. I could feel it.

"Too bad. He sounds so much nicer than Filipe."

As soon as I walked into the buffet, my waiter from yesterday's breakfast stopped and smiled. *"Buenos dias, senorita."*

"He's good," I whispered to Camille and lifted two fingers to the man called Jorge, still surprised that he remembered me.

"Si."

We followed him as he glided through the buffet, where enough food to feed several armies over awaited the resort's hungry guests. He led us to a table outside where he pulled out our chairs and carefully placed linen napkins across our laps before offering us coffees.

It was warm and breezy, and the humidity was starting to rise, however, we were sheltered on the west side and for now, this area was cooler. Netting hung from the ceiling to the deck rails, presumably to keep out the birds chirping nearby, but it offered a decent view of the sea, if you craned your head hard enough to the left.

"They have great food here." I pointed to the huge buffet, just in case Camille had somehow missed it as we strolled past.

"Great." She dismissed my comment. "Tell me more about Jon."

"There's not too much more to tell you. He's very sweet."

"I got that." She rolled her eyes and played with her hair, tying it up on the top of her head. It was always perfectly messy, the way it's supposed to look.

Mine always resembled a Pinterest fail of a messy bun. I just couldn't get the messy part of it right. It was either too ballerina-like or absolutely wild, like an afterthought.

"God, I can't believe you haven't even kissed him. If it were me …" Yeah, they would've done the tango in the sheets multiple times already. But that was Camille, not me. "Is he here? I need to see this guy."

I glanced around, seeing no one familiar. Not even his friend Irwin. "Nope."

"Oh, well." Camille smiled as a couple of tanned guys swaggered by, one of whom was making wiggly eyes at her. *"Buenos dias."* Coming from Camille, it sounded sexy and sultry.

The taller of the pair of good-looking guys paused

and winked at her. "Hello, there."

Camille lowered her head and giggled while covering her mouth.

Oh. My. God. It was so cliché I wanted to gag. And yet, it worked. Every. Single. Time.

He pointed his finger at her in a gun like fashion. "See you later? At the infinity pool?" With a wink, he took off.

"Geezus, Camille."

"What can I say? He's a fucking hunk. Do you have extra sunscreen? I may need to borrow some." Like a hot guy didn't just hit on her, she rose and stretched. "I'm going to eat."

I was still drinking my *café* and enjoying the relaxed atmosphere when Camille set a full plate of food down. "I hope you have some protein in there somewhere."

"Under the pancakes, there's eggs and bacon. Don't you worry, I'll burn it off." She put a chunk of syrup-soaked pancake into her mouth.

"Probably, but do me a favour today? Go easy on the drinks." Lately, she'd been a little more liberal with her alcohol, nothing at a level I should worry about. Yet.

"Hey, the drinks are free."

"Nothing is free. Everything comes with a price."

The food on her plate looked appetizing and my stomach growled in protest. "I'll be right back."

The other section of the restaurant was busy; people of all ages, nationalities and sizes mingled around, checking out the variety of delicious smelling foods. Following their lead, I grabbed a clean plate and circled around the buffet, doing a test run to see what I wanted to start out with first.

"May I suggest the tamales?" Jon's arm bumped mine, sending a flight of butterflies swirling in my stomach.

"Good morning," I said shyly, channeling my inner Camille. It worked, and I was rewarded with the sweetest grin that pushed up the corners of his deep blue eyes. "Tamales, eh?" I wasn't sure if I wanted to attempt something spicy so early in the morning. I didn't need anything to tamper with my colon while out on the ocean later. Still, not to seem boring, I put one on my plate. "I have something for you. Back at my table." I pointed out toward the terrace where Camille sat, not that Jon knew who she was. There were so many people standing between me and her, she was impossible to see.

"You have something for me?"

"Yeah. I'll come find you when you're done breakfast." I glanced around the area. No Irwin in sight.

"Unless you're dining alone?" Secretly I hoped he wasn't, because I wanted to spend time with Camille and felt it would be odd to invite him to join the pair of us.

"Actually, I am. My friends aren't known for being up this early."

"It's after nine."

"I know." He winked. "Where are you sitting?"

"See the beautiful blonde out there by the railing? The one with a top knot." I pointed again, hoping Camille would sense that and look over and wave. My ESP was clearly broken.

"I see a blonde, but she's talking to a guy."

Damn it, Camille. That girl was oversexed, if that was even possible. A revenge cheat was one thing, but it was like Camille was out to avenge every wrongdoing Trey had ever done. Wonder who the flavor of the day was now? "Yeah. That's her." I tried to keep my voice light while the strange guy took a seat beside my best friend. "Come join us." May as well, didn't look like it was just me and my best friend.

"Love to, give me a minute to load this up." He added a few more items to his plate while I did the same.

I walked back to my table while keeping an eye on Camille. Her laughter punctuated the air as she tipped her head back and closed her eyes. She was such a flirt. The guys had to see it was an act, I was sure. It was so obvious.

I interrupted her soft giggle. "Camille, I'd like you to meet, Jon."

"And I'd like you to meet … I'm sorry, what was your name?" she asked the model-worthy guy sitting in my seat. Said with the sweetest tone, I was getting cavities.

"Dom."

"This is Dom," she said for my benefit, and shoveled in half a pancake. Her long, manicured fingers tapped the folded piece of paper under my phone.

Right, the whole point of inviting Jon over. I lifted it and gave it to him while I sat in another chair. "This is for you." Somehow, by the grace of God, I managed to keep my excitement tempered.

Jon sat as well, setting his plate square in the middle of the place mat. He opened the papers and his eyes went wide. "How did you? They were all booked up."

My gaze quickly fell upon Camille. Would it seem desperate if I told the truth? I didn't want him to think that of me, or to think I'd use his impending disability to get a deal.

Camille jumped in and waved her hand around. "They were mine. I booked when we checked in and decided I didn't really want to go." She touched Jon's hand with a sigh.

"That's ... Wow. Thank you. It's very nice of you." He gazed upon Camille with a look I was unfamiliar with—as if he could see right through her. However, Dom cleared his throat and Jon pulled his hand out from under Camille's. "I wonder if Irwin is up to changing his plans?"

My heart splashed into my stomach and stopped beating. How foolish had I been to think he'd actually ask me? I jabbed my fork into a piece of mango.

"Ah, forget Irwin. He and Jacy will probably be busy." He tapped my hand. "I don't suppose you have plans for tonight?"

My heart fluttered back into a natural rhythm, and a flush crawled over my chest at the thought. I took a pensive breath, no need to act rushed. "No, I don't think so."

"Great. Let's make it a date."

"A date ..." I stammered out. Sure, I'd been spending a lot of time with Jon, strolling the boardwalk and gazing out at the stars, but an actual date? Suddenly, I was over the moon filled with excitement.

Chapter Seven

Camille pinned the last piece of my hair in place. "Perfect. You look amazing."

For once, I couldn't disagree. I stared into the mirror and was impressed by the brunette looking back at me. Hair *expertly* piled up in that messy yet vacationy way. The sunshine had warmed my skin and with a flick of bronzing powder, I didn't look so pasty white anymore. Or burnt. The makeup on a whole stayed minimal though.

"Don't forget this." She placed a white wrap over my navy blue tank top. Somehow it added to the outfit and didn't make the white jeans look so out of place. "Gorgeous. Now go and have a good time."

"What're you going to do?"

"Well, Dom's having a party in his room tonight. And Chet said he's going to the show on the other side of the resort, but that sounds boring as hell. Who the hell comes to Mexico and watches a play? Emilio said he's going to the bar, so that's a possibility."

"Who are these guys, and where are you meeting them?"

"Well, Dom is the guy from breakfast."

Yes, I didn't forget him. Seemed kind of douchy and cocky.

"Chet was that cute guy in the speedo at the swim-up bar and Emilio is the bartender."

Seriously. We'd been here two days and she had three new boyfriends. The revenge meter was climbing rapidly. "Text me at all times and let me know where you are."

"I'll be safe." She gave me a kiss on the cheek. "Promise." Pushing me towards the door, she stopped. "You should pack a condom. Just in case."

"Camille!" Heat seared my cheeks. "We're going out sailing. And I would never."

She shoved one into my purse anyways. "Yeah, but you should. It's fun." The door clicked closed behind us.

I arrived on the main floor and scanned the open-air area for Jon. When I spotted him, he was already fixed on me, but it was me that couldn't take my eyes off him. Wearing khaki-coloured cargo shorts and a green button up, casually leaning against one of the stone walls, he was a runway model if ever there was one.

"What, no bathing suit and a book?" he asked with a smile as he approached me.

It was true. Today had been a lazy pool day for me, drinking and splashing around when I got too hot and needed cooling off. Just being around Jon was enough to warrant a constant cooling off all on its own. We hung out poolside until Jon had to leave at one, and then I just read and enjoyed not getting sunburnt. Judging by the nice bronze glow I had, I think I was successful.

Jon, who was already nicely tanned, appeared even darker than this morning but it suited him. "Bus'll be here in ten."

"Perfect. I can't wait. This is going to be so much fun."

"May I?" He extended his hand, palm up.

"You may," I said suggestively, trying to channel Camille's flirtatious nature. My hand slipped into his warm one, fitting perfectly. Like a bolt of energy hit me, my heart reacted and sped up to a dizzying level. It was hard to believe how much my body responded to him, and it had only been thirty hours.

We strolled around the main lobby, stopping at the excursion board set up by the airlines.

"Can I help you with anything?" The lady behind the desk rose to her feet and clasped her hand in front of her.

"Just looking."

Jon tapped the board. "Booked this for tomorrow morning." He pointed to the quad ride. "And figured, why not do the zip-lining the next day?" His handsome face turned towards me. "Why don't you come with me? It could be a lot of fun."

And holy, fricking scary. No way was I going to go zip-lining. Not the adventure I had come to seek out in Mexico. "I think I'm busy."

"Oh, yeah? Reading? Swimming?" His tone was as light as his wink. "Come on. Come with me. It could be nice having someone snuggle against my back on the quad."

And me wrapping my arms around you. Wait a minute, what? What was going on in my head? "The quad ride is maybe doable. Maybe." A charming smile greeted me, and melted away my reservations. Afterall, I was Jessica the fearless, not Tess the fearful. "What the hell? Why not? Just not the zip-lining."

His smile twisted in a mock pout. "Aww ... I'd meet you on the other side. To catch you. I've never zipped over a jungle before."

The lady at the desk pointed to the picture. "If you're worried about safety, it's all good. We're very stringent about our safety record."

It wasn't the safety issue. At least part of it wasn't. "I'm not sure."

"Tomorrow morning, is there space in the ATV tour?" He pointed to the quad excursion.

She typed quickly. "It's all booked."

Silently, I screamed in joy.

"However …"

My stomach twisted.

"If she wants to ride on the back with you, we could accommodate her for a very small charge. It would be way less than a full fare."

"What do you say?" He gave me puppy dog eyes and the sweetest smile I'd ever seen.

With a nod and a flash of his credit card, we were booked for the trip. Just like that.

"C'mon, we're being waved to the bus." I pulled on Jon's hand. That was more my style. Casual, relaxing. I wasn't sure what to expect from a ride through coconut plantations on the back of a four-wheeled ATV but I highly doubted it was calm.

The bus ride was quick, as we were the last resort pickup, and we arrived at the marina in under ten minutes. Our tour guide escorted us down the dock and over to a giant catamaran, listing gently on the ocean. There were limited seats, and only in the middle.

Jon looked like a ghost as the colour faded from his face.

"You okay?"

His gripped tightened unexpectedly around mine. "I wasn't expecting this. Thought it would be like a yacht or something. This ... There's no railing."

There was. Sort of. More like a water-ski-type rope all around the perimeter. "I'm sure it's safe. There've been no accidents or anything." And I would know. I checked all the reviews I could find. Everyone had great things to say about the sail, with some even recommending it as the highlight of their vacation.

He gasped. "There're no life-jackets."

Except that. That surfaced in a couple of reviews. It's not that they didn't have life jackets per se, just that they weren't handed out. Unless you truly felt better with one. Like the one lady already on the boat pulling the tacky orange float around her neck. That was probably why no one wanted to wear one. They were awful looking.

Jon's hand turned cold wrapped around mine. I

guessed he was more afraid than he was letting on and it was kind of endearing.

"We'll be fine. I promise." I gave his hand a squeeze.

He inhaled sharply and nodded.

Slowly, we inched onto the catamaran and found a place near the middle, but not on a bench. Instead we sat right on the floor, like many others were doing. Surprisingly, it felt more secure than the steel and wood benches looked. Jon sat beside me, eyes darting everywhere.

"Do you want a life vest?" I whispered, not wanting to draw any unnecessary attention our way.

"You promised you'd save me." There was something in his voice that led me to believe there was a double meaning in his words, but I wasn't going to push it.

We were on the Pacific Ocean, nearing sunset and I was about to set sail with a gorgeous man. Seriously, if anyone was being saved, it was me. I linked my fingers through his as the captain opened the sail and we floated away from the dock.

The sail was smoother than I expected, and the captain was great at pointing out various things that we couldn't see from shore, such as the caves in the two small volcanic islands west of our boat. The sail closed and we drifted around, everyone taking a few dozen photos, myself and Jon included. The sun was dipping lower between the two islands, and it promised to make for a truly magical picture.

I scooted to the edge of the boat and removed my shoes, tossing my legs over the hull. We were high enough up that unless a hard wave hit, my feet were going to stay dry. Still, I loved the feeling of being *that close* to the water, and hearing the smaller waves smack the sides.

Jon inched up behind me and cuddled in, putting his legs on either side of me. "Does this bother you?"

I shook my head and leaned back into him. It felt perfectly natural. "Check out all the colours dancing on the ocean." The way the sunlight hit the water, it caused a bright narrow V of brilliance to contrast sharply against the dark hues of the water. Tips of white on the peak of a wave caught the sun, but in a breath, they were gone.

He wrapped his chilly hands around my waist. "And the texture of the rocks. Even from here they are quite jagged and rough."

I imagined climbing it, although not very high, would be a tough trek with some serious gear. If you fell or slipped just a little bit, you'd be gifted with a nasty gash. There'd be no way to avoid it. Volcanic rock was quite hard; beautiful and breathtaking, but unforgiving.

"Want to know a fun fact?"

I smiled. "Sure."

"This is the area Andy Dufresne escaped to."

I faced him, curiosity ripe on my face as the setting sun. "Why do I know that name?"

"He was the main character in *The Shawshank Redemption*."

"And this is where he came?" I remembered there being a beach with a boat at the end of the movie, but I didn't remember it looking like this.

"Yep."

"How cool is that? We're on a movie set." I laughed and focused back on the lowering sun. It truly was picturesque as it dipped between the two islands, slightly off centre as we drifted.

Jon rested his chin on my shoulder and his gentle breaths competed with the waves splashing against the hull.

I snapped a dozen more photos and the start of the sunset. In a panic to get the setting right, I hit the camera flip button and it was centered on Jon and I. That beautiful ear to ear smile stared at me as he beamed into the camera, tipping his head toward me. I did the same and clicked. The glow from the sun cast a warm and heavenly colour over us, making us appear healthy and dare I say it, truly happy? I flipped the camera view back and refocused on the imminent sunset.

The sun inched lower and lower, and the crowd on the boat stopped chatting. This was what we all came for. As the sun prepared to say goodnight, the most magnificent shades of orange filled my field of view and I found myself holding my breath. Warm hues of burnt amber hovered above the horizon, and the dark silhouettes of the islands softened to the point where the jaggedness disappeared. The sun lowered itself gently into the darkening blue of the ocean depths. Slowly and slowly it sank, until a flash of green shot out before its final plunge.

"Oh, my God," I breathed out. "Did you see that? That green flash?"

"I thought it was something wrong with my eyes."

"They say," said the tour guide who spoke from behind us, "once you've seen the green flash, you'll never go wrong in the matters of the heart." He barefooted away without another word.

I turned to face Jon, to take him in before the darkness settled over us. This man, a stranger less than two days ago, was as magnificent as the sunset. Charming and real, and breathtaking. He was taking me all in as well, like he was seeing me in a whole new light. The air between us was highly charged, and he tipped his head toward me.

I leaned in and brushed my lips over his, softer than I expected and yet, there was a firmness in the sweet caress. Until he pulled back, I didn't know I could become addicted after just one touch. I wanted more, and my whole body craved that wondrous sensation.

The sail flapped open once again, and the captain chatted about many things found in the area, but I couldn't hear him clearly over the rush of my beating heart. That moment with Jon was one of the most romantic in my life, beating out the proposal I'd accepted several months ago.

With Filipe, there was love, but no butterflies, no pounding of the heart. If there had been, it faded very quickly as I didn't remember it. With Jon, a mere look sent my heart soaring, the butterflies launching themselves into a frenzy, and my breathing fought to stay calm and controlled. However, I reasoned with myself that it was all lust. I'd only just met Jon. He couldn't be *the one* because he lived way too far away. All this was was a week-long fling, if it was even that. Just someone to hang out with, who happened to be as charming as he was good-looking.

Still believing it was all a dream, I pressed my back into his chest, and his arms securely held me to the boat rather than let me float into the air. We rode back in silence. A comfortable silence.

Chapter Eight

I found Camille with another strange guy, and the two of them were playing billiards in the games room. Poor guy didn't know he was up against the Gator Lounge Tournament winner, but I was pleased as punch to find her all the same.

Immediately, she put down her cue stick and held up her hand in a pause motion to the guy, before scurrying over in my direction. "Heeeyyyy," she sang out. "How was the boat trip?" Jon and I still hadn't unlocked hands and her focus zeroed in on that, her eyes going wide as saucers. Camille's gaze roamed over me, studying me like I was a foreign biology term back in high school.

I smiled at Jon with a tipped head, and glanced back to my best friend. "It was good."

Her whole face lit up in shocked disbelief. "Good? That's it?"

I shrugged. As if I was going to spill here, right

now in front of Jon, about how fucking incredible it actually was.

Jon twisted and whispered in my ear. "I'll go grab us a couple of drinks. Cabanas?"

"Why not? Thanks." And for the first time that evening, my hand suddenly went cold, and I became lonely.

Camille watched as Jon walked away and flipped her gaze back to me. "Oh my God, girl. What happened to you? You are positively glowing." Her hand waved up and down my body. "You've never looked so lit up."

"Yeah." My heart sank a little. A week-long romance was all I was going to get. Jon lived too far away to make anything work, if that's what he wanted. If it was even what I wanted. I didn't even want this originally.

The tall guy she was playing with strode over and positioned himself behind her. "Hey, are you coming back? I'm waiting."

"Yeah, yeah, yeah." She picked up her stick and wiggled her ass into him. With a quick aim and slide, she sunk the cue ball. "Whoopsie." She covered her laugh. "Guess that means *game over?* Now, where was I?" She sauntered over, her hips swinging from side to side. "So, tonight was wow, eh?"

I nodded and a smile bubbled up across my face.

So much for keeping it all under wraps. "Camille, it was amazing."

"You're falling for him."

"Not possible. I won't let it happen."

"Ha-ha. Tell your face and maybe scream it at your heart." She wasn't mad, just the opposite. Camille knew what I'd gone through with Filipe and how much that whole nasty situation had destroyed me. I hadn't come here to find love. I'd come to escape the hate.

Jon came back and handed me a pink drink. "Here's your drink, Jessica." He linked his fingers back through mine.

"Jessica?" Camille mouthed, narrowing her gaze.

That's right, I'd forgotten how I missed telling her that I'd given him a fake name. It was no big deal in my mind. Besides, maybe Jon wasn't his real name, although I knew it was. The name on his credit card was Jonathan Baker III. The third. A little pretentious, wasn't it? Or was it? I really knew very little about the man aside from his vision issues and a bit about where he currently lived.

"So, Jon, tell me. What are your plans for when you go home?" Camille asked point-blank, and I nearly spit my drink all over her.

He glanced from me to her and back to me again. "Work like a dog, I suppose." He tilted his head to the side while pursing his lips at my best friend. "Is that what you mean?"

She stared at our locked hands. "I mean relationship wise. Is there someone waiting for you back home?"

Leave it to Camille to not beat around the bush. I wanted to be angry and shush her, but I was too curious to his answer. Guess maybe I should've checked that beforehand. With my intense bad luck with members of the opposite sex, he was probably a first-class player.

Jon rocked back and forth on his heels and let out a huge sigh. "The only one waiting for me back home would be my dog, Twink."

Yes, he was a dog person.

"I see." Camille still didn't look impressed, which was kind of ironic considering how many guys she's flirted with, and I knew for a fact her and Trey were an item. Maybe not a good item if she was having revenge sex with every guy she met, but still. "There's no lingering relationship? No girl that got away from you?"

I cleared my throat. "Camille, that's enough."

"I'm just asking, is all."

"I think he's answered. Let it go." I gave her my best stop-it-right-now look. It worked. Camille backed off. But it was too late.

The mood between us changed and Jon remained a little further away, drinking his drink and staring at anyone but Camille or me. He'd even let go of my hand. "Oh, there's my friend. Will you excuse me for a moment?"

I turned and followed his gaze, spotting Irwin in a heartbeat. "Yeah, absolutely. Go." I wanted a moment alone with my friend anyways. Especially now that she'd ruined what had been the most incredible evening of my life, or at least this trip.

"Actually ..." He checked the time on his watch. "I should probably get some sleep. Our bus is picking us up at eight tomorrow."

"Bus? For what?" Camille asked, leaning a little harder on her pool cue turned walking stick.

"We're going quadding." Jon answered before I could.

"Really?" She gave me a curious look and mouthed in my direction, "Who are you?"

He planted a quick peck on my cheek. "See you in the lobby in the morning?"

"I'll be there."

Jon sauntered away from me, probably glad to leave Camille behind, and I twisted my attention back to my best friend.

"What's wrong with you? Why'd you ask all those

questions?" I pulled her over to the side, away from the pool table area.

"'All those questions?' I asked him two." Her thin eyebrow rose uncharacteristically high.

"But why?"

She rubbed my arm. "Because you're my best friend. We came on this trip to get away, to leave your miserable life behind."

"And I'm trying to do that," I said through gritted teeth.

"By going on a sunset sail and quadding? With a guy you don't even know?"

"Yes. Precisely. I'm stepping out of my comfort zone. Big time. I'm going out to do things I never thought I would." And right there, I decided. Fuck my old life, I'm going zip-lining too. Why not?

"You sleeping with him will be stepping out of your comfort zone. All this other stuff, it's all fluff." She crossed her arms over her chest and sighed.

It was true. I'd only ever been with three guys my whole life. Filipe being the most recent, and even that was some time ago.

"I know you're trying to get over Filipe, but is Jon the right person for that?"

"Jon is exactly the right guy. He's everything

Filipe wasn't, and Jon's not even trying that hard. At least I don't think so. It feels …" I inhaled the spicy aroma of food cooking and suddenly I was hungry.

"Yeah?"

"Never mind." It's way too early to even be thinking about the feelings Jon was bringing out in me. Way too early.

Camille waved her hand in front of my face. "Filipe was a jerk. A huge, monumental jerk, and everyone knew it but you. EVERYONE. You fell so hard and fast for him that you blocked it all out. But it was there, and I don't want this guy to hurt you the way that douchebag did."

"I promise." Going forward, I would try to put a safe zone around me.

"And don't even get me started about that bitch at your old office who enjoyed rubbing Filipe's indiscretions in your face."

"Yeah, I know." My mood was souring by the second. It felt like a lifetime, when in reality, it was less than eight weeks ago. I thought back to Tina. She had been quite flirty whenever Filipe showed up to take me home, but I thought she was just like Camille, and it was part of her nature. She did seem to flirt with anyone and everyone. However, the truth rolled out. Quite literally. I came home early on one of my weekend shifts and caught them rolling around in our bed. I kicked Filipe out immediately, didn't even give him time to shower. Camille came over right away and we packed his stuff, bed sheets included, and dumped it all on the lawn. Trashy, I know.

But the work environment was the worst. Filipe, having no place to go, actually moved into Tina's place, and she made sure I knew about it. Of course, she also painted me as the evil one, even though it was *my* relationship she wrecked. She snapped at me whenever I was near her and accused me of stealing away her clients. The boss didn't like the unhealthy negativity so I got shuffled to the bottom of the work schedule, and we were put on different shifts. But it wasn't enough. Eventually I just got tired of the gossip and backstabbing and hearing about how wonderful my fiancé was in bed, so I quit. When I go home, I'll be starting over with the new job. I'd already moved into a new apartment just a couple weeks prior.

"I love you, Tess, and I don't want you to hurt like that ever again."

"I can promise you it's not going to happen. I'm just having a little safe Tess fun. It's harmless."

"Is it?"

It had to be. Jonathan Baker the Third was a stranger, relatively speaking. My heart wasn't ready for anything more than fun, and it wasn't even sure if it wanted to be a part of that. I just wanted to relax, enjoy the sun and try not to think about my life back home. Jon was merely a distraction, and a damn fine specimen at that.

Chapter Nine

My heart was heavy as I descended in the elevator. All night long I'd tossed and turned, my thoughts constantly focused on Jon. Slowly, I was growing attached to him, but I had to push away. Or, in my moment of brilliance, just go hard for the rest of the week, knowing it won't last after he's boarded his plane back to Maine. However, I wasn't sure I could separate my heart from my mind, they were too interconnected. Channeling Camille's advice sounded easier in thought than in practice.

I stopped by the excursion desk and booked my zip line trip. Why not? I was here to be the adventurous Jessica, and this would be an epic adventure. If the crippling anxiety didn't kill me first.

A throat cleared behind me, and with my ticket in hand, I stepped off to the side. "Oh, good morning."

Jon stood before me in long pants and a long-sleeved T-shirt, wearing sneakers. Hardly the attire for a day out in the sun.

"You know it's going to be super hot today, right?" I planted my hand on my hip.

"It was suggested on the itinerary to wear this." He stared at me hard and filled in the blank he must've thought I didn't get. "For the quad trip?"

I gave myself a once-over. The quad trip was through a plantation and across a beach, that's why I was perfectly dressed in a tank top and short shorts with flip flops. "I'll be fine," I said with an air of confidence. "I'm riding on the back of an ATV."

He grinned, the left side of his face reaching higher than the right. "If you say so." He glanced to the paper in my hand. "What did you book?"

"A couple of things. Guess who's going zip-lining with you tomorrow?"

"Please tell me it's not your best friend?"

I laughed because it was funny, but it really wouldn't be. In fact, I'd be a little terrified for him having to spend two hours listening to Camille rant on and on. Or worse, having him fall under her flirtatious charm. Playfully, I smacked his arm. "No, me, silly."

"I like the sound of that."

"And," I said, keeping the best for last. "I hope you don't mind, but I booked something truly incredible. A turtle release for the day after."

"Seriously? We were told that they weren't going to be ready yet."

"Apparently, the sanctuary says they are." Or I just wasted a ton of money for the experience of hoping to see baby turtles.

"When?"

"We go Thursday." His second to last day here. "It's an afternoon thing. I hope that's okay?" Maybe it was presumptuous to have booked this without asking first. Maybe he wasn't really interested in going with me. Dang, I should've thought it through more. I stared at the extra ticket. Camille wouldn't be the ideal guest to join me, but it would be better than going alone.

His face tightened, and he rubbed his temples. "Man, I really want to go. When would we get back?" He turned and asked the lady behind the counter.

"The bus returns for seven."

"Seven. Seven." He tapped his head with his finger while he closed his eyes.

Had I overstepped? I thought it would be fun. I've always wanted to do something like that. It's marginally out of my comfort zone, as we're taking a bus to a location fifty-five miles away. To a *remote* location where there's no cell phone reception. Although it doesn't involve any daredevil activities, it's still brand-new to me. However, if he can't make it, which judging by the way his brows were furrowed tightly together it was a strong possibility, I was taking Camille.

"It's no biggie. If you can't make it, Camille would love to come." At least I'd have two days to prep her for this. And it was an afternoon event, no worries about waking early or tucking in early.

"Bus is for sure back by seven?"

The lady nodded.

"Okay. It doesn't give me much time to clean up, but it's doable." Finally, he gave me a passing look and a nod. "Great." A smile crossed his face. "I think it will be a lot of fun."

"If you have other plans, it's okay. Honest." I really wanted to do this with him, but I understood. Whatever other activity he had planned, it seemed pressing.

"I do have very important plans, but this'll work. I'd rather spend my time with you anyways." His smile was so genuine and sincere it made my heart flutter. "C'mon, Jess. Let's take you quadding."

Ninety minutes later, a little shook up and dirty, our quad tour pulled into a Mexican village whose name I couldn't pronounce. We rode through the heart of their space, stopping at a thatched-roof restaurant.

Our tour guide hopped off his quad and waved us to follow him inside.

Jon hopped off first and extended his hand to help me off. The black vinyl seat stuck to my skin and the first layer ripped off when I stood. Jon snickered as I gave my back side a rub.

"That's part of the reason I wore long pants."

"Yeah, well ..." I pulled off my bandana the tour guide had provided each of us to cover our noses and faces with. There had been no mention on the write up that it was going to be such a dirty mess.

Jon did the same and after removing his sunglasses, there was a very distinct dust line where his glasses had protected his face. The trip had been dusty, but I didn't think it was that dusty.

"Let me help you." Jon reached under my chin and unbuckled my helmet, slowly pulling it off.

What hairs weren't plastered to my head in sweat, stuck to the helmet. Awesome. I tried giving them a fluff, but it was pointless. I couldn't even imagine how awful and gross my hair looked.

"Doesn't matter what you do," Jon said, setting the helmet on the seat, "you're still beautiful."

Well, damn. I moved the shoulder strap on my tank and gasped. Yep, I had dust lines too. Super attractive.

"Beer time?" Jon tipped his head toward our rest area.

"Definitely."

We entered the open-air restaurant, something that still caught me off guard. We needed more of these establishments back home. It was cool and breezy and yet, perfect. Our tour group was sitting at the back, the ocean just feet behind them. Beers and snacks were set in the middle and everyone was helping themselves and digging into the bowl of fresh chips and guacamole.

As I reached the back, I stopped and stared. The beach at the edge of my feet was endless in either direction, almost a whiteness to the sand. It was so different than the beach at the resort. Here the waves were bigger and held more power and mystique, and a much bigger pull for me to run through.

"How long are we stopped for?" I asked the tour guide, a solidly built man with skin like leather. Back home, he'd definitely pass as a biker dude.

"Thirty minutes."

I grinned and widened my eyes as I turned my focus to Jon. "Can I go play?" It was such a childlike request, but I just had to. Sitting on the back of a quad all morning, driving through trees wasn't very exciting. Maybe if there'd been headsets in the helmets telling us what we were seeing, it would've been more fun. Instead, it was relatively boring as I couldn't tell the difference between a palm tree and a coconut tree and a cocoa bean tree. Everything looked the same. The only highlight was seeing the donkey who'd stopped the tour as he was blocking the road.

"Sure. Have fun."

I waved and jumped off the raised platform, leaving my flip-flops on the edge of the wooden floor. The hot, sunbaked sand nearly scalded my feet, but I didn't care. I ran out to the ocean and along the edge where the water met the sand. It was cooler there. Heavenly. I kicked at the water and watched as the rivulets of water washed away the dirt and dust from my legs. Cupping my hands, I poured handfuls down my calves, giving them a solid rub for good measure and cleaning them up nicely. A little sand mixed in helped scrub away the remaining dirt.

"You're cute, you know." Jon sauntered over.

"Thanks." I straightened myself up, still gently kicking the surf. I'm sure somewhere in a past life, I had to have been a fish or something. Being in the water calmed me instantly.

He passed me a paper towel. "For your face."

I dampened the towel and squeezed it out, patting my face.

"Let me help." He took the towel and gently wiped under my eyes and down the bridge of my nose, taking the dirt off in the most seductive way. Rewetting the cloth, he brushed it over my forehead and gave my cheeks a pass. "Look at all those freckles." The tip of his finger tapped each one in succession. "You're really something." He dropped his hands into the water, rewet the towel, and gave his face a quick, manly scrub.

Seeing how he'd removed his sneakers and socks, and rolled up his pants, I playfully kicked a little water at his legs. Not too much as there was no need to soak him.

He stood and a devilish little smile crept across his face. "Whatcha do that for?"

I turned and sprinted away, splashing my feet as hard as I could in the surf, not giving a rat's ass if I got soaked or not. There'd be time to dry. Quickly I stopped to see where Jon was, and he bulldozed into me, sending us both careening into the water.

I was laughing so hard I couldn't catch my breath.

"You okay?" he asked, rolling off me. In defeat of staying dry, he just laid on the sand, waves racing up to him and retreating.

Finally, I replied. "Oh, definitely. You?"

"I'm soaked." He curled up into a sitting position and, crawling over just as wet, I dusted away as much sand out of his hair as I could.

"You're cute, you know."

Even from under the sunglasses, the sparkle in his eyes was visible. Unable to stop myself, I leaned forward and kissed him. He responded and cupped either side of my face, tenderly at first like I was fine china, and then he put more passion and fire into a kiss than I knew was possible. And fuck me, it undid something deep in my soul and this time, I was the one who pulled back.

A quick glance at the restaurant and everyone was staring at us.

"We should dry off."

We checked out the group. One guy raised his beer in a cheers-like fashion.

Jon straightened up and dusted himself off, but the fleece material of his sweatpants held onto the water and sand like a magnet. It wasn't going anywhere. Perhaps during the rest of the tour, it would dry somewhat.

I looked down at myself to see what a mess I was. It wasn't any better. My tank top stuck to my bra, revealing the lines of where the half-cup held up its payload. My stars. I fanned my top a bit.

We approached the back end of the restaurant.

"Wait …" I grabbed my purse and removed my phone, tossing it to the tour operator. "Can you get our picture?"

Jon scrunched up his nose. "Looking like this?"

"Yeah. We're happy, aren't we?"

He wrapped his arm around my waist, and I did the same while we leaned our water and sand heavy heads together.

"Done." The tour guy gave me my phone, and I checked out the picture. It couldn't have been more perfect if it had been planned. The endless blue ocean, the white sand and a goofy looking couple wrapped together. We were definitely a mess, and yet somehow, it was the best photo of me I'd ever seen. There was zero doubt that, in the moment, I had found my happiness.

Chapter Ten

"Oh, my God, that was the best." I stepped out of the van that brought us back to the resort.

The driver rolled up the towel I'd been sitting on and gave it to me. He did the same with Jon's, which was heavier as he was still wet.

After our impromptu dip in the ocean, we'd climbed back onto our quads. The tour guide told us the beach was ours, and we were to head to the outcropping five miles away where the sandy beach met the desert. One by one, our group revved the engines and drifted at high speeds through the sands.

Feeling safe and secure, I'd encouraged Jon to open 'er up and give 'er. He did and I'd screamed in joy, throwing my hands in the air as he throttled it. I'd even managed to snap a picture at his top speed just to prove to Camille how fast we went. The salty air in my face, driving through the edge of the ocean, and wrapping my arms around Jon made for a pretty amazing return trip to the tiny little Mexican village.

We tried to sneak through the lobby, dust covered and dirty, but the visitors stared us as we waited for the elevator. We must've been quite the sight. Jon rode up with me, and we stopped at his floor.

I got off with him and stood in the hallway. "I'll see you later?" There was hope in my voice for more. Maybe dinner? Drinks by the rolling surf?

His dust-covered hand squeezed mine. "Meet you for supper?" He kissed the tip of my nose.

"Sure. It will give me time to catch up with Camille." And show her the pictures. She'd never believe it.

"I agree. I need to check in with Irwin too."

"You really should shower first though," I laughed.

He stepped over to the side of the elevator and checked himself out in the mirror. Water-logged sweatpants hung around his hips, and his long sleeve shirt clung to his chest, defining its musculature. His fingers brushed through his dark hair, grains of sand falling on his shoulders. "Well, that explains the staring."

"Ah, whatever. No one here knows you." It's not like I looked any more put together. At least I was avoiding a reflection. No need to see that disaster.

"Aside from Irwin, Jacy, and your friend, Camille."

"Aside from them," I smiled. It was hard to walk away, but for now, it was what we should do. I pressed the up button. "Thank you for the day. I had a really good time."

"I know." He tapped his ear. "It's a good thing we were wearing helmets. I might be deaf from the screams of delight." He bridged the distance between us, which wasn't much to begin with, and pulled me close. His lips brushed against mine, and I parted them, giving him permission to enter. He did not disappoint as his velvety tongue searched out and explored.

Between us, his desire for me grew hard and pressed into my hip. And I wanted to explore it further. "Grab a change of clothes and come to my room." The breathless words were out of my mouth before I had a chance to stop them.

The elevator chimed behind me and the doors opened.

He pulled back and gave me a solid look, as if he couldn't believe what I just said. "You sure?"

"Absolutely." I stepped away from the elevator and followed him to his room.

Two minutes later, we were unlocking the door to

my room. The maids had already come by and left a fresh assortment of towels on the vanity, and a lovely swan on the bed, surrounded by roses. I tossed my bag onto the floor without further delay.

Jon dropped his clean clothes on the edge of the bathroom sink. "Shall I help you out of these dirty clothes?"

"Yes, please," I practically begged.

He reached his arm around and pulled me tight into him, kissing me and devouring me in such a way I could've orgasmed right on the spot. Slowly, he tugged on the hem of my top, taking it over my chest and up over my arms.

"Damn," he said, as he bent down to kiss the swell of my breasts, barely encased in their holdings.

My breath held onto itself. Those lips of his, warm as ocean air, soft and gentle as a billowy cloud. My eyes closed for a heartbeat as he cupped the underside of my bra. Returning back to earth, I took in the sparkle and desire in his pools of blue. I struggled a little more removing his stuck-on shirt, but Jon assisted in pulling it off since he was taller than me. It hit the floor with a thump. His neck was two toned; one with dust and dirt, and the other a golden bronze. I put my hands on the waistband of his sweats and inserted my thumbs under to give me leverage.

"Are you sure?"

I gazed into his dark blues. "There's nothing I want more." And it was true. Had there been any reservation, I would've hesitated. But there wasn't any. Every fiber of my being wanted this. "And you?"

"Oh, yes," he whispered into my ear, sending tingles of electricity to places I didn't even think would be erotic zones. "I need you, baby."

I stepped back, scrunching up my face. "Just please don't call me that." It brought up images of someone I'd rather not see.

"Sorry, Jess."

That didn't help either, but that was on me. At least it was better. My thumbs touching the soft skin beneath his sweats, I pushed down the thick, damp material. Jon stepped out of his pants wearing boxers with ducks on it. I supressed a giggle, and refocused on his mostly naked glory. Fuck, was he gorgeous. I was going to enjoy kissing every square inch of his perfect body.

"That look you're giving me," he caressed the side of my cheek, "is a huge turn on."

It was hard not to tell as I glanced down, and witnessed the built-up presence. It electrified me and sent pulses of energy to the ends of my fingertips.

He reached behind me, but I held up my hand.

"Allow me."

A groan fell out of him as I unhooked my bra, and slowly, tantalizing him, slipped the straps off my arms and held up the lime-coloured undergarment before I let it drop to the floor. I loved the feeling of standing there, in my half-nakedness, while he took me all in. I expected his gaze to linger on my breasts, but instead, he held my eyes with his, as if he were caressing them. It made me want to melt.

My hands slid over my chest and down to the button of my shorts. The button popped and I unzipped them slowly, opening them up and revealing my pretty pink polka dot underwear. Had I known this was going to happen, I would've found something that matched. Too late now. I shimmied the shorts over my hips, keeping my gaze locked on him. Seductively, I turned my body around and stuck my thumbs into the waist of my panties.

Jon stepped forward, his erection pushing into the fleshy part of my ass, while his hand slipped around my waist then lowered between my legs.

A deep guttural groan moved through my body.

Both of his hands inched lower, one finding my pot of gold first, the other only a heartbeat behind. Feeling his touch, my breath caught in my throat, but new energy hummed through me. The deeper he explored, the more intense the emotions ravaged me. I lifted my leg and placed it onto the lip of the tub, giving him easier access to a place no one had visited in a long time. Expertly, he found the sweet spot and brought forth a rush of sensations that I'd thought were long dead. They were heady, and instinctual, and very much rising to the surface.

"Don't move," he whispered and suddenly dropped below me, the top of his head coming up between my legs.

Oh, good God.

Sweet, sensual kisses travelled up the insides of my quivering thighs to the sweet cave in the middle. Firm yet tender fingers stroked and glided before his hot breath and velvety softness pressed against me. Every heated touch pushed me one step closer to a total explosion, so I leaned at an awkward angle to brace myself against the countertop for fear I'd collapse on top of him. I think it only gave him better access. For the moment his tongue dove deep inside me, a crescendo of epic satisfaction washed over me. I shuddered and shuddered, revelling in the totally euphoric feelings pulsing through my soul. Heat rippled from my core, and like a wave on the sand, washed over me, tinging my skin a flushed colour. I stepped back and set my foot on the floor, hoping I had enough strength to stand. I needn't have worried.

A crinkle and tearing sound came from below and the condom wrapper flew into the garbage can beside me.

Jon stretched himself taller and wrapped his strong arms around me. With little effort, he lifted me up, carrying me a few steps to the giant walk-in shower. He twisted the faucet on and cold water shot through the shower head and hit my back.

I gasped, the pleasurable mini-earthquakes disappearing in a flash of blue.

"Sorry. It'll–"

I didn't give him a chance to finish and claimed his sweet-tasting lips. He pushed me back against the tiled wall of the shower, under the spray of the showerhead which was warming up as fast as I was.

He angled me and slid me lower against his torso. The tip of him poised and ready to find shelter.

"Take me," I breathed out and nuzzled my lips against the scruff of his chin while my hands wrapped around the tautness of his neck.

And take me he did. If he was aiming to shoot me to the moon, he underestimated how much I'd missed this kind of a connection. His hands held my ass and I wrapped my arms around his neck. Never had I been at the mercy of someone's strength. All I could do was hold tight and enjoy the ride, and it was the best fucking ride of my life. I landed amongst the stars.

Too many never-have-I's washed down the drain

that fine afternoon. Jon made a woman out of me more times than I could count, each one taking me to a higher and higher level. I never knew a shower could be so fun and I actually enjoyed the lengthy process of getting suds up and rinsed off.

Satisfied, and borderline exhausted with breathless fulfillment, we turned the water off and reached for fresh, dry towels.

I wrapped mine around me and sauntered over to the balcony. With his towel around his waist, Jon followed me and placed the two deck chairs side by side.

Another glorious sunset was on the horizon, and our energy was spent, so in silence we sat and held hands as the sun blew good night kisses at us. We did not see a flash of green this time, but I felt the flash when I looked over at him.

He was not watching the last dance of daylight. Instead, his focus was on me. "You are truly beautiful. One of a kind."

My cheeks were too worn out to blush, but they would've if they could've. "Thanks. You're pretty darn spectacular yourself." I turned my building smile back towards the ocean. "Aren't you going to watch?" And commit another sunset to memory?

"Nah. I already saw the most amazing one

yesterday, and nothing holds a candle to that. For as long as I live, I'll remember it in every single detail." He trailed a finger down my cheek. "Just like I'll remember these tiny little freckles all lined up in a row. Reminds me of Orion's Belt, and they are placed just as equally apart." He tapped the three beauty marks on my left cheek that I'd always found rather odd in their placement.

"What's Orion's Belt?"

"The things I could teach you about the stars." He shook his head in mock disappointment. "Ever hear of the constellation of Orion? It's one of the most popular sights in the night time sky."

"It sounds vaguely familiar." I shrugged, trying to recall any lessons from science class that would help me out. "Was he a Greek story too?"

"Of course." His dimple deepened and he swallowed. "Orion is often depicted as facing the charging of Taurus the Bull or pursuing the Pleiades Sisters or chasing after the hare called Lepus."

"Which do you believe?"

"All of them. When you see him in the night sky, he's quite magnificent and all those constellations are there. But the best thing about Orion, is his belt."

"Oh, really?"

"Yes." He faced up into the darkening sky and

lowered his voice. "For if you look closely, you will see something truly remarkable."

He had my full attention, and I leaned closer while holding my breath.

"Right below his belt, there is a nebula, and within that nebula, something is happening that's never been noticed before."

"What's that?" I asked, my voice barely audible.

"New life is beginning. You see, a nebula is what's left over after a star explodes, and it takes a long time to see the beauty of the changes ahead. The start of new life. New dreams. It's all there in Orion's Belt." He tapped the three freckles on my cheek.

Suddenly, they had a whole new meaning, one I took straight to my heart.

Chapter Eleven

The scent of BBQ and something else delicious wafted up the side of the building, tempting my senses. Despite the very personal astronomy lesson I was getting, my stomach protested a lack a food and growled quite loudly.

"I'm hungry. You?"

Thankfully, Jon's growled louder. "Starving."

He dressed in a nice pair of shorts and a simple tee that bore an image of KISS.

"Big fan?" I pointed to the logo.

"Not at all. Irwin dragged me to their concert. Figured it was something I needed to see before … you know, I can't." His voice trailed off.

My heart was breaking for the guy. So many things to try and commit to memory so later in life you could recall it with amazing clarity and detail. It was a shame how many people took their sight for granted.

I gave his arm a gentle squeeze. "So, why'd you buy it?"

"Guilt?" He shrugged. "Regardless, it's a nice material. Feel." He pushed his bicep in my direction.

Pinched between my fingers, I gave the fabric a rub. "Top notch."

"See. There's a plus in everything." He pulled me to the door. "But we can discuss this over food. Seriously, I'm starving, and …" A quick pause to glance at his watch. "If I don't get downstairs to meet up with Irwin, he'll have my head on a platter."

"What's the story with him?"

"What's the story with your friend?"

"I've already told you. She's my best friend."

"Mm-hmm," he nodded.

"Hey, I just proved to you how into guys I truly am. Above the bath, in the shower, on the vanity." A smidgen of disbelief circled my brain that I had done the deed so many times over a small amount of time, and with a guy I've only known for a relatively short spell. I crossed my arms over my chest and mock pouted.

"I know. I'm just giving you a hard time." He placed a sweet kiss upon my cheek. "I'd love a repeat though, just to confirm things." The most charming wink came my way as he spoke.

The door clicked behind us, closing in a wonderful memory. I wanted to commit it all to heart, every last word. That's what my journal was for and I intended to fill it full later tonight.

Jon's phone buzzed, and he read the display before dropping it back into his pocket. "I need to go and take care of some things."

It was probably for the best, even though it pained me to be away from him. "I should try to track down Camille anyway. I'll follow you to your room since that's how we met in the first place." I winked and held his hand all the way to his room.

He dropped his key card into the slot and the light flickered green. With a twist of his hand, he turned the knob. "Perhaps I'll see you later?"

"If you can find me."

"Challenge accepted." He darted his gaze both ways and gave me a kiss that meant business. I'd experienced a few of those over the afternoon. "If I fail in meeting up with you tonight, meet me in the lobby tomorrow at eleven. And wear comfy shoes, clothes, and for the love of God, put some sunscreen on." He entered his room and closed the door.

For a moment, I stood and listened, hoping that would give me some kind of clue as to why he needed to go so urgently. Not that he didn't have a right to. He'd been with me all afternoon. And that was amazing. But his friends needed to see him too.

I knocked on Camille's door and waited. No answer. She was probably at the bar, or in the games room. Alone, I wandered around the resort. It was peaceful, but I felt strangely out of place. All around me were couples and families. Soloists were nonexistent.

Taking a deep breath, and a bold move, I coasted to the boardwalk and down the lit path, my sandals flopping against the wooden boards. There was a breeze upon the air and on it floated the most amazing scents. With my nose as a guide, I followed the savoury smells over to the oyster bar and grabbed a table for one.

While dining alone, I jotted down all the memories from the day into the journalling app on my phone, recalling every sweet and tender moment, along with the times where my breath was taken away. As I went, I inserted pictures where appropriate and snapped a few more from my corner table of the oceanfront restaurant. The journal got a little longer each day, and when I returned home, I'd be able to print out my own little vacation story into a coil bound book. I was having so much fun, I didn't want to go home. And the most fun definitely had Jon's name all over it, mixed with the romance. That was the hardest part, knowing that it was over come Saturday morning. Time needed to slow down.

Camille and I managed to meet up the next morning. I banged on her door until weary and hungover, she finally answered. A part of me hoped Jon would question the incessant knocking and I could see his handsome face, drunk with sleep, but he never answered.

Instead, I dragged Camille's sorry ass down to the buffet and we sat in Jorge's section.

"Eat," I said, pushing her plate of bacon and eggs and fruit towards her.

"Not really that hungry." Still, she twirled her fork around her plate and gave her puffy eyes a rub.

"I think what you need is a day in the pool. To relax and stop boy-chasing for a bit." Last night, after my solo dinner, I'd headed back to the lounge area and spotted Camille with a small group of people. Like a stalker, I'd sat where she couldn't see me. I'd kept an eye on her, not wanting to join in on the billiards game nor the dancing, but to make sure she was safe. Camille was drunk, but pleasantly, she wasn't stumbling and maintained control. She'd even headed up to her room alone just before midnight, or at least got into the elevator by herself. "And maybe go easy on the drinks for the day."

"Maybe," she shrugged. "But the drinks are free."

"And so's the food. Doesn't mean you need to eat all day long."

She stuck her tongue out at me. "Spoil sport."

"Yep. Whatever, I'd rather be a spoil sport than an enabler."

Camille dug into her plate of food, cleaning up her plate in record time. She headed to the buffet for round two.

I finished off my meal, sticking with the easy-to-digest foods. With today's adventure coming quick, my stomach was already tossing and turning, no point in giving it something that would settle like a lead weight. It would be best if my stomach was empty before I departed.

Camille returned with a mountain of food. Seriously, where did it go? Her metabolism had to be sky-high.

"I still can't believe you're going zip-lining. You. The one who's afraid of heights and yet asks for the top-most floor."

"Because there is ground underneath me on that top floor, and I can handle the view. When zip-lining, my legs will be dangling."

"You'll chicken out, and then Jon will find out

you'd been lying to him about being an adventure seeker." She scooped up some eggs onto her fork and had a bite.

"He won't find out. Besides, the only thing I've kept hidden is my real name. Big deal. Everything else has been me. And it's only a few more days, today, tomorrow, Friday and he's out of here first thing Saturday. Just like you." And then I'd be on my own for three days. I had no idea what I was going to do with my time. Maybe something a little more Tess and less Jess, perhaps even finishing one of the three books I'd brought. Whatever was going to happen, it would either be really good for me or would be the most boring time ever spent. Time will tell.

I drank up a cup of coffee, and Camille grabbed a third plate of food, this one all fruit and chips with salsa. I stole a chip, and filled it with the homemade tomato/cilantro/jalapeno dip and popped it into my mouth. Holy spicy. That would help run everything through your system. One was enough, and I left the rest for my friend.

With the sunscreen lathered on good and thick, I spread out my towel on my chair and lay on it, tummy side down. It was high time I got some colour on my backside. I readjusted my bikini bottoms as the waiter walked by.

"Excuse me," Camille called out.

I gave her a stern look.

"Can we get a couple of waters and two of those?" She pointed at the table next to us. It was like a cabana but instead of a solid pink colour, it was three colours in layers; pink, blue and white.

"Ah, a Pacifico, *si*." A quick nod as he left me behind and collected drink orders from the other sun bathers.

I was into the first chapter of my romance book when he returned. I dropped a fifty onto his tray and gave Camille her only drink of the morning. "No more until noon."

"But I've eaten. You saw that."

"Yes, I did. Still, take it easy please. For me?"

She grunted and slowly sipped her drink. Probably was killing her to nurse it.

Chin on my arms, I people watched as I had direct line of sight out of the adults only area and toward to the main pool where everyone else seemed to be hanging out. People watching was always interesting to me, and if it were a subject taught in school, I'd have honours in it.

It was borderline addicting to imagine what life was like for everyone when they weren't here being catered to. The family of four, where the mom was chasing after the toddler and the dad sat on his phone ignoring the chaos, were they like this at home? Or was this irregular, and he was checking work emails, and their nanny was on holiday, so the mom had to child-mind? It was utterly fascinating to me. I watched a variety of different groups of people and couples, giving them a life back home that may or may not be true.

But one of them caught my eye. Let's be honest, Irwin's hulking size was a presence not to be missed. He had his back to me but sat on the edge of the pool. A young lady, who had to be half his age at least and a fifth of his size, pulled herself out of the pool. But it wasn't the stark contrast in size that commanded my attention, it was the handsome guy coming out of the pool. The one who hopped onto the ledge, water dripping off his perfect body, and leaned into the young lady, who cupped his cheeks and planted a wet one on his lips.

What the hell?

I nearly scrambled off my lounge chair and pounced over, but I couldn't make myself move. Was there something about me that made guys cheat on me? Pushing up onto my elbows, I scrutinized them like an eagle on his prey. There were no further kisses, and no touching either, but that one kiss bothered me.

Camille rolled over and poked me. "What are you staring at?"

"Him. Jon."

"Oh." She rolled onto her tummy and stretched her neck across my chair and peered in the same direction. "Where?"

"Over there. By the big guy and small lady. He's on the side of Little Miss String Bikini."

"Big deal. He's here with friends." She moved back onto her lounger and repositioned her head to stare at me.

"She kissed him." My voice pitched. I glared at the woman, not that she would see it.

Camille, however, did. Sighing, she closed her eyes. "I'm sure it's nothing. Innocent. Friends kiss each other." She waved a finger between us. "We've kissed each other. Big deal." She cocked her eyebrow. "You're reading too much into this."

I exhaled. Maybe. Unlikely, but maybe. Is that how Filipe had started? Just an *innocent* kiss?

"Besides, what's the big deal? Are you suddenly a couple and I missed the memo?"

Maybe? I don't know. We've been having such a magical time with each other. My heart had started thinking there was something there, but the more logical part of my head knew it was all over in a few days. My focus returned to the threesome. Figured I would've read more into the relationship or whatever it is that we had. Would be just my luck too. Finally find someone whose company I enjoy, and he'd been two-timing me. Jerk.

Camille pulled her floppy hat low over her eyes but not before giving me the side-eye. "If you're so concerned, ask him. Aren't you two hanging out this afternoon? Grill him on it. Don't make assumptions and let some sort of miscommunication ruin the fun you're having." She stretched out. "Or maybe this is the sign that it's time for you to move on to someone else."

Yes, it was only a week-long fling, but deep in my heart I knew I didn't want my fun to be with anyone else. It was Jon's company I enjoyed. He stoked things inside I hadn't felt in a long time. Not even with Filipe.

But I couldn't help wonder if I was just a fling to Jon. Maybe this was something he did all the time. Jet off to some exotic location, wine and dine some bored beachgoer and leave. Maybe it was all just a game to him. When he said he wanted to see everything, did he mean different ladies too?

My chin dug into my forearm as I watched him and the cute lady interact. They were close with body contact, but not over the top. At least not from my vantage point but it was still enough to toss gas on the embers of jealousy. It was a constant battle to remind myself that I wasn't his and he wasn't mine, and this whatever-it-was was only for a week. Whatever happened between us couldn't logistically happen after we left. Two different cities, two different countries. It would never work after Saturday.

I woke up angry, and my skin was more than a little pissed off as well. My butt cheeks were tender, and since they don't normally get a lot of sun, I was truly sore where the sun doesn't shine. Damn. Hey, maybe it was the perfect excuse to get out of zip-lining?

Wearing shorts that ended mid-thigh and a halter-style tank top with my long hair in a tight braid, I paced around the entrance to the resort waiting on Jon and wearing a path on the sidewalk. The shuttle driver was impatiently waiting for Jon, who had failed to arrive. About ready to give up, I headed back into the lobby in time to spot Jon rushing through.

"Sorry. I was tied up."

There was a mental image I didn't want. At least not if it was done by mystery pool lady. If anyone should tie him up, I certainly wouldn't mind. What was I thinking? I pushed the thought out of my brain. He wasn't really mine, was he?

"Ready?" He tugged on my hand.

I really wasn't and had hoped the shuttle would've left without us, and yet, two minutes later I was driving through the Hotel Zone on our way to meet what would probably be my death.

There was so much on my mind, so many things I wanted to ask Jon about that lady, but on the shuttle bus full of other tourists, it wasn't the right place. Instead of talking, I gazed out the window as we drove through the elaborate and well-maintained tourist zones into the desolate and run-down areas of the locals. It was a stark contrast between green and riches, to dirty and barely scraping together two pesos. It tore at my heart strings.

At a red light, a little girl of five or six with pig tails, stood on a corner, tears running down her eyes and holding a sign asking for money. And I wanted to open my wallet, reach through the window and give it all to her. I'd only packed a couple hundred pesos, but from the conversations I'd had with Jorge, that would be a small lottery. It was a hit to the heart of how truly blessed I was to be so well off, and I wasn't rich by any standards. At least not where I came from.

I hadn't realised my own tears from watching the little girl had snuck out until Jon wiped them away.

"You nervous?"

Well, I was, but that wasn't the cause.

He stretched out over me and looked out the window. "Ah," he said, falling back into his seat. "They know what works, don't they? Try not to let it bother you. It's an act."

I blinked away the rest of the tears as the shuttle lurched back in its takeoff.

He carried on. "My cousin works in Central America, and this is a bit of a con. They select the cutest child and make her stand out there with tears and the saddest face known to mankind. Usually they can cry on command. The kids make a fortune from the tourists too. Upwards of a thousand pesos a day. And that little girl, she doesn't get anything. It's child abuse."

I twisted back to the little girl, but she'd run off and I couldn't see her. "Really, it's all an act?"

"Works, doesn't it? It's a good way for them to make a living, and tourists eat it up. Tourism is their economy after all."

So much to learn.

He squeezed my thigh. "Seriously, though, you okay? You've been awfully quiet and that's not like you."

I resumed my blank stare out the window, the barren trees a blur. "I have a lot on my mind."

"Anything you want to share?"

My eyes met his dark blue ones and held the curiosity and questioning in them. This just wasn't the place. Later. I shook my head. "Not now." First, I needed to figure out how not to make it an inquisition. Or maybe find out first what was going on between us. If it's truly nothing, then I was getting worked up about nothing. And that was pointless.

The bus rolled over a gravelly road and parked under the canopy of a giant tree. One by one, the adventure-seeking tourists with broad grins filed out and swarmed over to the waiting tour guide. Wish I had that much excitement.

My heart pounded a little too hard as I searched out the area behind the eager group. Tucked above the tour guide, a hundred feet up, a wire cable was visible, stretching its end far out into the jungle. My throat resembled a dry desert, complete with tumbleweeds, and I dug through my bag in search of a water bottle. The warm water did little to soothe.

Chapter Twelve

After a brief safety tour where I committed to memory every last detail I'd ever need, I got fitted for a harness, the guide tugging and tightening the rigging. "Make sure it's snug." I repeated that phrase at least a dozen times but I wasn't ready to face certain death. At least not from the apparatus.

The climb up the rickety stairs to a small platform and over a long wooden suspension bridge was exhausting. Had I not been ready to throw up from anxiety, I would've enjoyed the view more. My legs were like jelly, my knuckles white from their death grip, and I struggled to form coherent sentences with anyone.

Our first terrorizing zip line station lay ahead at the end of the bridge I struggled to cross over. Not because the bridge itself scared me, but for what awaited me when I stepped onto the wooden platform; a ledge surrounded by a rope for protection. It resembled a poor man's Swiss

Family Robinson treehouse. I stood on the platform—the first of twelve as I was reminded by some asinine fool speaking behind me. This ledge wasn't as high as the one at the entrance, but it was high enough that I was overlooking the tops of a few trees and many shrubs.

People clipped on and sailed effortlessly, peals of cheers and good-natured ribbing aplenty. Lucky bastards.

"You go ahead," I told the older lady behind me. "I'm still just readjusting." I tugged at my left leg harness to prove my point.

She clipped her rigging on, and the operator gave it a double-check, and off she went like it was second nature to fly. I honestly believed if God wanted us to soar, He would've given us wings. And I didn't care that a fifty-year-old woman had no fear of flying, as I sure as hell did. The edge called out to me, but I couldn't force my feet to walk any closer. There was way too much air between the ground and where I stood.

"You're up," Jon said as a pulley returned. Damn him and his charm. He was thrilled, and even behind the sunglasses, I could see how his smile pushed up the corners of his eyes. I wish I had a tenth of his excitement.

I checked to see who else to go ahead of me. There was no one left. I'd let everyone go already. Damn.

Hands shaking and heart pounding so loud I

couldn't hear the operator clearly, I inched to the edge and handed him the clip. *I can do this. Oh please, let me do this without dying.*

"Closer," the operator said, and gave my harness a little tug.

This—I studied the tiny contraption that was supposed to hold me above the ground—was sheer stupidity. This wasn't a brave thing to do. This was idiocy at its finest. It was designed for people not like me to enjoy. I wanted nothing more to do with it. My mind was changed, and I shook my head. "Nuh-uh."

The operator tugged a little harder.

NO! I screamed the words in my head and wrapped my arms around my chest. I went to sit down in protest, but the adrenaline coursing through my body managed to override common sense. Like an idiot, I pulled my feet up, and without warning, I was suddenly airborne. My arms flung out to the sides, wavering all over while I bounced above certain death. A scream, uncontrollable and ear-splitting, rattled me right to my core and broke apart something inside my soul. My head felt light and my body twisted without rhyme or reason. I worried that my heart would actually break my ribs from the incessant pounding it was giving. Yep, I was dying and this was the way I was clocking out of this world.

With a sudden jerk, I swung forward and backwards, and a strange voice said, "You here."

I opened my eyes and immediately set my feet on the wooden platform and hugged the guy. I was alive. I'd been so sure that I was free falling to the ground.

He unclipped me and I collapsed, my legs had zero strength.

Behind me in a blurry haze, Jon laughed and sailed with his arms wide open. He looked like he could fly or was at least trying to. Effortlessly, he stepped onto the platform and unclipped, like he'd done this a million times.

"Hey," he said, squatting down and rubbing my knee.

"I ... I ... I ..." I gave a pretty solid sniff and wiped the back of my hand under my nose. "That ... That ..."

"That was the most imaginative way I've ever witnessed anyone zip line." He said it so sweetly, I almost smiled. Almost. "As long as I live, I will remember it."

"I ..." My breath felt like it was trying to strangle me.

Jon sat beside me and unbuckled my helmet. The rush of cooler air over my head was unexpectedly calming. "Just breathe." He clipped his sunglasses into the V of his shirt, and gently pinched my chin between his finger and thumb, tilting my head up to make eye contact. "Just breathe, Jess. In and out."

I focused on his eyes, on the dark blue ring encircling the lighter ocean-blue iris with starburst flashes of green and grey shooting out from his pupil. His left eye had more green and the right had more grey.

"There you go. See." The edges of his eyes turned skyward.

A strong inhale of air went into my lungs and ballooned them out, and slowly, I released the air, strength rushing back to me.

"If you were truly that terrified, you shouldn't have gone. You should've said something before we were harnessed." There was compassion in his tone, for which I was thankful. At least he wasn't upset with me.

"I tried."

"Yeah, well lifting your feet was a bad idea." He smiled as he spoke.

"How far was that? A hundred feet?"

We both looked over at the other platform where two people were harnessed up and ready to fly.

"More like fifty."

"Seriously?" However, it was fifty feet more than I expected or wanted to do. Wait until Camille heard about this.

"Come on, we'll climb down and wait for the tour

to finish up. Rumour has it they make the best mango salsa here." He pulled me to a stand.

My legs were still akin to wet noodles, but they had some minor stability which made me walk like a newborn deer. However, the back of my legs were burning from the pressure of the straps against the tender, charbroiled skin. I gave them a quick rub and tugged on the harness.

"How do we get down?" There were two cables, one extending in each direction.

"That ladder." Jon walked to the operator. "We're going down."

The operator unhinged the latch in the floor marked emergency escape and held it open. Ladder was a poor description. These were planks of wood nailed to the tree trunk inside a rope tube. It was a toss-up as to what was the safest way and my gaze flickered between the 'escape' via a hole in the floor or the zip line of death. I gazed over at Jon who was trying hard to hide his feelings. Sadness and disappointment crept over his face, and it killed a part of me knowing I was responsible for putting it there. Try as he may to be a good sport about it, having the best salsa in the world wasn't what he had in mind.

"You came here to experience the beauty of nature, and to see it all in its glory."

"And I can see it all from the ground too." He

hovered over the hatch. "Besides the view from the rope bridge was pretty amazing."

"Why don't you go on? I'll watch you from below. Plus, I'll be able to get some really great shots of you."

He inched closer to me and whispered in my ear. "I'm not leaving you alone here."

Well damn. I had two options. Take the coward's way down and ruin the experience for Jon, or find a way to curb my fear and make this enjoyable. The second option didn't seem ideal, but practicality aside, it was the only option. It was a long way down on the nailed-in planks.

I scanned the length of cable to the next platform. It was about the same distance. Fifty feet apparently. I survived the first one, barely, maybe the shock of the whole thing will be less the next time?

"Let's go. Let's do this." I put my helmet back on and tightened the chin strap.

"Jess, you don't have to. I didn't say what I did so you'd do something that frightens the hell out of you."

I swallowed as I checked out the cables and met the concern in Jon's eyes. "If you meet me on the other end, it will give me something to look forward to."

"I can be here and let you go."

I shook my head. "No, I don't want to leave *you*.

I'd rather you catch me." In my head, that had sounded more romantic, but as the words spilled out it came across as cheesy and desperate.

However, his response was what I'd hoped for. He beamed and checked my chin strap. "You sure?"

A rush of air filled my lungs and a surge of adrenaline raced through me again. That gut-wrenching pukey feeling settled in for another round. "Absolutely."

"The lady says we're staying," he told the operator who dropped the hatch. The platform vibrated with the thunk. "This time," he said to me, readjusting his own harness. "Pull on this if you want to slow down." He reached up and pointed. "Watch."

The operator ensured he was secure.

"Kiss me first," I said, before he pushed off.

"With pleasure." Lips, soft and sweet, pressed firmly into mine. They moved with a promise of more, and that was something I couldn't wait to experience again. He pulled back and gave me a nod before releasing and sailing through the air. Thirty heart-pounding seconds later, he touched the catch at the other end.

Lungs shivering and my brain in a giant fog to recall all the lessons on safety the guide went over, I inched my toes closer to the edge. Hands shaking worse than before, I handed the operator my clip. A roving check and

I was ready to go. Palms sweating, I reached up to the trolley and held on as if my life depended on it.

"One, two …" I closed my eyes and lifted my legs. This time I groaned deep and instinctually as my stomach plummeted into my feet, but I didn't scare the birds out of the trees. Silently, I counted to seventeen as I pulled on the trolley. At eighteen I opened my eyes and standing on the platform with the biggest smile ever, snapping pictures, was Jon. At twenty-eight, my feet touched the surface.

His lips found mine as his arms encircled my waist. "You were great."

And it was easier. Even I smiled. But only at the end. That whole stomach dropping out of me feeling wasn't as intense on the second trip as it had been on the first, and for a micro-second, it just may have been an enjoyable ride.

Chapter Thirteen

Well, I'll be damned. By time we got to the fifth cable, I was able to sail with my eyes open and take in the beautiful scenery. We were prepped that the seventh line would be the longest, just under a kilometre, which doesn't sound like much until you're sailing through the air with nothing more than a few straps suspending you above the tree line. Then it felt never-ending.

"You are doing so well," Jon said with gusto as my feet touched onto platform #8. "You're a natural."

I laughed.

"Are you having fun?"

"You know what, I am. I'm not saying I'd rush out to do this again, but for a brief moment in time, I can tolerate it."

"We're getting near the end." He hung his head a little, and sadness crept over his face.

I felt the same way. The end was near. But not of the zip line tour, of my adventure with Jon. However, I'm pretty sure that's not what he meant. Still, I nodded. I had so much I wanted to ask him and tell him and correct. But it would have to– "Hey, do you see that?" I pointed to the top of the tree beside us. A little monkey head had peered out and was staring at us from one of the branches. Jon's wish came true.

Jon lowered his voice. "Oh, my. He's so cute."

Indeed. That dark and hairy face with beige fur around his black, piercing eyes was adorable. I could just put that monkey into my pocket and take him home.

I watched Jon from the corner of my eye as he stared at the monkey. Was he watching the way his tail swooped and how he rubbed his jaw with his cute little monkey paw? What details was he trying to record and preserve? My fingers found his and wrapped through them tightly, savouring the way his slightly damp palm pushed into mine. He blinked rapidly while he scanned the treetops and every so often, a gentle sigh blew out of him. I wanted to record all the details of him to my memory, but I wasn't very good. However, my camera was, and I took a few dozen pictures, and perhaps a selfie or two with him.

With the tour all finished, thank the heavens, I stepped out of my harness and passed it back to the tour operator, finally free to move without the worry of something pinching my ass. We grabbed some homemade chips and "world-famous" salsa and sat on a picnic table.

"Thank you for today, for everything you did."

"Today's not over," he winked.

Oh God, if that didn't set my soul on fire. I took a deep breath. "I want to ask you something, but I'm not sure how to ask without it being rude or tainted with venom."

"'Tainted with venom?'" He cocked an eyebrow. "What could you possibly want to ask that could be so bad?"

If you only knew. I swirled a deep-fried chip into the salsa and scooped it up. "Well, there is quite a bit I have on my mind."

"I've always believed in honesty being the best policy, so whatever you are concerned about, just spill it."

If it were only that easy. I crunched the chip and rather enjoyed the taste of the salsa. A little heavy on the cilantro, but otherwise, yeah it was a damn good salsa. Wouldn't say best ever, but decent enough. I stared at the man sitting across from me, mindlessly eating his well-earned snack.

"This morning, before we left, I saw you at the

pool. With Irwin and ... a lady."

He tensed up and his chip stopped in midair.

The words fell out of my mouth in rapid succession. "And I know we're not a couple or anything. Actually, I don't even know what we are. Camille says it's just a week-long fling and come Saturday we're each going to go our separate ways and never hear from each other again. But I think it's more because you say all these amazing things that sound like they're coming from the heart, and it's not just lip service. But …" I inhaled a quick breath to further me on. "When that lady kissed you, it twisted something in me, and I didn't like that jealous feeling it stirred. I've been through enough back home, and I don't want to go through that ever again. I won't allow myself to be walked all over. But it all circles back to—"

"Whoa, slow down." He pushed his plate of food off to the side. "There was a lot in there." A sigh fell out of him. "What to start with. Okay, that lady in the pool, shall I address that first?"

Shrugging, I nodded. "It's probably the easiest." I removed my hand from the top of the table, resting it in my lap.

"Yes, it is." He held my gaze with his own. "I guess I haven't said much about Irwin and Jacy, have I?"

I shook my head. At least now I had a name for the

woman. Tension radiated out from my shoulders down to my fingertips, causing them to curl tightly into my palm.

"Irwin is a longtime friend of the family and a surrogate big brother. He's as big in personality as he is in size and tends to go overboard. Doesn't help that he's highly protective of me."

Irwin had nothing to do with my question, but it was nice to know his connection to Jon. "And the girl?" Because he still hadn't got to that.

"That's his fiancée."

"Hmm …"

He carried on, without a glance at me. "Jacy's very affectionate with me, and I know what you must be thinking."

I highly doubted that.

"But I swear, we've been broken up for a long time. She's marrying Irwin."

"What?" That wasn't what I expected.

He rested his forearms on the table and leaned into them, head tucking down. "Years ago, when I was fresh out of college, we had an affair. It didn't last long, but we remained friends. Good friends. When I got the diagnosis about my vision, and the breakup came, her and Irwin stuck by me. They were the only ones."

I pushed myself forward, taking in every word. My

curiosity wasn't completely cured. There was still something he was withholding.

"I suppose I should back up that train a bit."

My heart did a double skip, wondering what was left to come. My nails were digging into my palms and I forced them to open up and stretch, even if for a moment.

"I hate talking about this part ..." His shoulders rolled forward.

"Three years ago, I was dating Amy. Then I got my diagnosis and things changed. Rapidly. Suddenly Amy started pushing for a wedding, and we'd only been going out a short while. She wanted me to see her in a wedding dress before I completely lost my vision. I hesitated on that as I hadn't yet proposed, I wasn't sure she was the one. Then came her self-imposed timeline with kids. Amy had it all planned out, assuming my vision deteriorated at the rate the doctor said. But it was too much. I didn't want all that, but she did. She was more invested in the relationship than I ever had been, or planned on. By that point, deep down in my heart, it was firmly cemented that she wasn't the one. Not by a long shot."

I held my breath. Wasn't I on the same path? Hadn't a couple of my dreams been as wild as Amy's? How I felt myself falling for him? Maybe he wasn't ready for me either, despite the fact I knew beyond a shadow of a doubt that once Saturday rolled on through, whatever we were would cease to exist, aside from some very intense dreams. Knowing that, something in my heart started to crack. How foolish I'd been to give into it. To let my heart lead. Putting the brakes on should've been a bigger priority.

"And you broke up?"

"Clearly." He pulled his hand back and resumed eating.

"I mean, did you break up with her or did she break up with you?"

"Does it make a difference?"

"Hell yeah."

He studied me and a pensive look crossed his face. "I broke up with her."

His heart remained intact then, because why wouldn't it? He was a guy. Amy and I were more alike than I thought. Jon's heart was going to stay one piece on Saturday whereas mine was already starting to splinter.

"And since then, have you had anything remotely serious?"

There was a hesitation, and he ate another chip. And another. "This will make me sound like a jerk, but all I've had is fun. A lot of fun. No strings attached. It's just easier that way."

And yep, that statement totally changed my opinion on him. He'd just cemented what I was. Fun. A roll in the hay. Another notch on the bed post. A quick poke, mess with my feelings and leave me kind of guy. And God, I'd been so blind it to too. His charming ways, his stories, the way he lured me in. Damn it. I really should've listened to Camille more and played the field. I came to Mexico to rest and relax and escape the assholes back home. What was so wrong with me that I attracted the worst of the worst? Why can't I find someone who was truly perfect for me?

"There was no point in getting serious with anyone after that."

"Huh?"

"Why should I? My vision's going downhill. No point in dragging anyone down with me. So many things are going to change, and—" There was a slight hitch to his breath.

A hardened part of me softened to the break in his words. "And anyone who truly loves you will adjust for you and makes things easier for you, because she'll want to. Because being with you is better than anything she's ever known."

He shrugged, and it instantly boiled my blood. It was a borderline confession of my feelings and with a simple shrug, he dismissed them.

I gritted my teeth and swallowed down the building bile. Words, any decent words, were now gone. I was so tired of being played. And I was done. To hell with coming clean about my name. It was all a ruse anyways. I was only his week-long fun.

I hunted all around for the perfect excuse to get away without being rude. I was better than that. At least in this moment. Besides, I'd caused enough scenes for today, and I wasn't interested in creating more.

The shuttle van rolled back into view, and an announcement came over the loudspeaker of the arrival.

"Well, that's the end of this." I rose unceremoniously. "Crap. I'm going to run into the gift shop and see if I can find something for Camille."

Jon dumped his plate into the garbage and followed.

Perusing the gift shop that was smaller than my hotel room, there wasn't much that related to the ziplining. A lot of it was junk and highly overpriced at that. At least there was no child standing with a street sign asking for money.

"What about this?" Jon held up a tiny skeleton keychain. What an odd thing to sell at a gift shop. A better time would be Halloween. "It's a lazybones." He laid it on the shelf and laughed.

My heart sank. If it hadn't been for that note slid under the wrong door ... But the keychain was perfect. For him. However, I couldn't buy him a gift when he stood right there. "I'll take it." The words were out of my mouth before my thought processes kicked in. "For Camille."

"It's because of her that we met in the first place."

My expression froze. "See, when you say stuff like that it makes things very difficult for me."

"What are you talking about?" A quizzical expression coloured his features, and he ran a hand through his dark hair and rubbed the back of his neck.

I shook out of his grip. "Never mind." At the till, I gave the lady payment and pocketed the keychain. My legs carried me back outside even if my heart and head wanted to stay where Jon was. It was pointless though.

"What's going on?" Jon nipped at my heels with his long stride.

"You wouldn't understand."

"Try me." He spun me around.

"I'm just foolish, and my stupid pride is trying to keep myself together."

"All aboard," the bus driver said in his best train conductor voice tinged in his deep Mexican accent.

I climbed inside and grabbed a seat near the front;

a place where I could sulk and stare out the window without having to make unpleasant conversation. It was best to cut the ties now. We were through. I was done being a toy. It hurt too much to be around him. Tomorrow I'd find someone else to join me on the turtle expedition, and Jon could *do* whatever or whoever he wanted.

Chapter Fourteen

It was a long, uneventful ride where an older lady sat beside me before Jon could and proceeded to give me her life story. Good thing a conversation wasn't required, as she barely came up for air.

As one of the first passengers to exit, I dashed out into the lobby, bypassed the elevators and headed straight to the pool area. It was before supper, and hopefully I would find Camille. I needed my best friend now more than ever. Sadly, she wasn't hard to find. I followed the roar of her laughter and located her in the adults-only pool, a couple of guys drooling over her.

One look in my direction, and she rose from her sultry position on the lounge chair, storming over to me, concern all over her beautifully bronzed face.

My legs gave out and I collapsed onto a concrete bench. "Oh, Camille. I screwed up."

"What happened?"

My hands covered my face and the hot sting of rejection wracked my body. It shook from the sobs.

"What did he do?" Camille's voice was firm and ready for a fight, but her arms were tender as she wrapped them around me.

"He … he …" It hurt too much to even whisper the words. And it really wasn't him. It was, but it wasn't. "I … I …" A moment of clarity surfaced and in it was the truth—Jon had made me fall in love with him and I'd allowed him into my heart. My lungs hurt to breathe, and I felt like I was going to snap in two.

"Oh, T-bird." One arm fell away and the other stroked my back. Camille cupped my cheek and turned my head to face her. Her blue eyes bored into me and in her searching, she'd found what I had been desperately trying to hide from myself. "Oh no. Tell me you aren't?"

I shrugged and pushed out of her hold. "I couldn't help it."

"It can't happen. He leaves on Saturday."

"No one knows that better than me."

"I told you to live a little, not fall in love with the guy."

"I'm aware of what you told me, Camille. Believe me, my heart is sustaining maximum damage right now."

Camille got in my face, but a small smile of

sympathy was there. "You're impossible, you know that?"

I nodded and sniffed. "Worst part is I knew going into this, that falling in love was out of the question. But somewhere between the sunset sail and screaming my head off as we zip-lined—"

"You actually zip-lined?"

"Jon has photographic proof."

Camille whistled.

Knowing Jon had been there and watched me conquer that fear but only did it because I was his brand of weekly fun caused another wave of sobs to wash over me. "I need you to see the big picture here, Camille."

"Sorry. So, what happened? How did you go from falling in love to this?" Her hand vibrated on my back.

"He basically told me I was just fun. That he wasn't going to commit himself to anyone."

"He said that?"

I nodded and gave my nose a wipe with the back of my hand.

Camille huffed and puffed out her chest. "Goddamn men are all the same. You give 'em an inch and they take the whole fuckin' mile, not concerned at all with your feelings." Her hands dropped to her lap and she gazed over to the pool. "At least you didn't have sex with him."

Oh God, the sex we had was amazing. The best

ever. I buried my head into my hands.

"You had sex with him? Have you not listened to anything I've said? Like ever?" She rubbed my arm, but I think it was to soothe her more than me because it didn't work. "I don't know whether to be downright pissed off or thrilled. Who are you?"

"I don't even know anymore." And that was the most truth I'd admitted to myself. Four days ago, I was a miserable girl, a follow the rules and play nice kind. You know, a genuine pushover. But here, I wasn't that girl. I embraced something inside myself that I'd buried for too long and stepped out of my comfort zone on a number of occasions. Instead of wishing I was an adventure-seeking person, I became one. And the best part? I was loving it too.

Camille rose sharply and stormed a few feet away.

Jon was on his way over.

She thrust up her hand and yelled, "Stop. Right now, mister."

Jon paled a little and glanced in my direction.

"I said stop!" Camille inched forward a little. When provoked, Camille could turn into a mother bear, I'd seen it before and right now, Jon was catching a small glimpse of it. It would be in his best interest to back up.

"I just want to talk to her."

"She's done talking to you. Go screw someone else." Her hand was up high, to his chest level.

He put his hand on it and pushed it down. "Do you really want to cause a scene?"

"I have zero issue with that." And I knew that was true. Causing a scene was like chocolate for Camille. There was always something satisfying about it. "Now, scram."

"Seriously?" He locked eyes with me and spoke past Camille, aimed directly at me. "I don't know what happened today but something changed. I want to know what I said or did because I keep flipping through everything and I'm coming up grey. Help me understand what I did wrong so I can fix it."

The words pulled me to my feet. Not that he could fix anything, but I hated hearing the anguish in his voice and seeing the hurt on his face and I wanted to put an end to it. They were slowly chipping away at the remnants left of my heart.

"Sit down," Camille said to me, and directed her anger at Jon. "All you guys think the same way and use that little head of yours," she pointed to his manly parts, "to direct your feelings. Well, not everyone thinks that way. Some people actually think with their hearts and you've done enough damage to hers."

"What?" His face crinkled in confusion, but he took a step back. "Jess, we really need to discuss this."

"She's done with you. You messed with the wrong girl."

"But tomorrow?"

Camille laughed, and it was the strangest laugh I'd ever heard. Borderline maniacal. "You actually think you're going with her to the turtle release?"

"She gave me the voucher." He put his hands on his hips.

Camille matched his body language and leaned forward. "Then I guess I'll be taking her place."

I couldn't believe my ears. Camille had told me there were a dozen other things she'd rather do than hang out with turtles.

Jon stared at her with challenge in his expression and I wondered how far this was going to go. Would he still show up? Would I have to cancel, or send Camille in my place? That wouldn't be fun for any of the involved parties, including the turtles.

Jon looked at me with hurt, and his pain was visceral. I sensed every part of it. "This isn't over," he said softly.

Camille stepped between us. "Oh, it's over, all right. And I should've put a stop to this a couple of days ago. I should've stepped in and said something after the sail. I saw the potential for hurt building back then."

My eyes went big as saucers, and with my best look, I implored her to keep her lips sealed.

But Camille ignored my pleading and spun to face me head-on. I was doomed. There was no stopping her now. "You are an overly emotional girl who wears her heart on her sleeve. You get emotionally attached to anyone who treats you decently, and this Jon is no different."

My legs weakened, and I crumpled back onto the bench and hid my face.

"What about that guy at the coffee shop who remembered your coffee order once and you were suddenly loyal to that location only, and him specifically."

Please, dust in the breeze ... Please take me with you.

"What about our waiter at the buffet here? Have you even sat in another person's section?" Camille hovered over me. "But the way you are, isn't a bad thing. It's what I love most about you. However, it's also the thing that prevents you from jumping from one guy to another the way I can. I have the ability to distance myself, but with you, it consumes your heart and you fall in love with the wrong fucking guy. The guy who toys with your emotions and has no qualms about it either." That was directed right at Jon. Her voice faded as she spoke to him.

How I wished the ground would tremor and shake and a hole would open up right there and swallow me in one quick bite. I didn't need to look to know that Jon heard everything. His footsteps retreated, and with it, he took away his fading sense of hurt.

"What if this was the right one?" I honestly didn't think that, but I was curious. Everything with Jon had felt so right and natural. Could I have been that mistaken?

"It isn't. It's wrong on so many levels."

"How would you know?"

"Because I've seen you go through this. With Filipe. Only this time ..." She pushed me over as she sat beside me. The sound that escaped her crushed me before her words could. "With Filipe, it wasn't like this. You were never this gaga over him, always content to do whatever he wanted, when he did. Like you needed permission. With Jon, you're still you, but like a rebooted version. And if an asshole like Filipe can destroy your heart, then I'm truly terrified that someone like Jon will destroy your soul. Even if you both only know it's temporary."

Chapter Fifteen

My chat with Camille did little to cheer me up. In fact, I felt worse when I went back to my room. I really should've listened to her and played the field a little, maybe the collateral damage would've been less.

How could I have fallen in love with Jon, especially at such a wicked fast speed? How is that even possible? With Filipe, we'd dated for months before I loved him enough to tell him, let alone had fallen for him. And the same could be said about him. I'd said 'I love you' first, but I don't know if he'd ever fallen in love with me. In the fallout of our relationship, I deduced he only asked me to marry him because it was convenient.

It was all so different with Jon. He was handsome, smoldering even, and the charm. Damn, a girl could really get used to that. I couldn't put my finger on what specifically he did, but everything he did to me and said to me lit me up from the inside out, and like the giant idiot I was, I bought into it. Hook, line and sinker. It was an act.

I filled the tub and opened the balcony doors. The fresh evening air was ripe with a sweet floral scent. A perfect escape. Nothing would be better than a long soak, listening to the merriment far below. I even turned off all the lights in the room but the light in the shower, which cast a surprising glow but wasn't too much. My clothes hit the floor and I kicked them off to the side.

A knock sounded on my door. "Housekeeping."

Damn, probably turn down service or a cool beverage refill. The hotel was adamant that bottled water was readily available. "I'm good," I said to the door. If I was out of water, I could pick up more tomorrow.

The knock came again. "Housekeeping."

Maybe they didn't understand English? I reached for my robe from the inside of the closet and cracked open the door.

The saddest looking guy I'd ever seen stood on the other side. "I need to do some housekeeping please." He eyed my bathrobe. "Can I come in?" A deep, broken voice rolled out of him.

I stepped to the side, but he remained frozen.

"Wait. Is Camille in there?"

"No. I left her downstairs."

His shoulders relaxed and he glided into the room.

"Am I interrupting anything?"

I closed and locked the door before I turned off the faucet to the tub. "No." Just a pity party for one; me and my misery for the night.

Jon held nothing back. "What happened today? I thought we were having fun."

"We were."

"And? Something changed, but I can't figure out what? Did I say something?"

I tightened my robe around my waist and stepped by him, sitting on the edge of the bed. The robe slipped off my legs.

"Before you say anything, can I ask you to get dressed? Or at least cover up more? Seeing you like that is putting fun thoughts in my head and masking my serious ones. And talking to you is far more important than doing you." He turned his head away from me. "Although, I wouldn't mind that. Later."

"Would pajamas be okay?" A nod of approval came from him, and I slipped into a pair of shorts and a tank top. "There." I sat back on the bed and studied his down-turned smile. No dimple was present. "You know what, you don't need to explain yourself to me. This problem, it rests on me."

"But that's the thing, I don't even know what I

should be explaining." He thrusted his hands deep into the pockets of his shorts and paced between the tub and the patio doors, stopping occasionally to glance out. "Are you upset about Jacy?"

Definitely not upset about her. If he says they were done, then I believed that. It's the part about not wanting to get involved again with anyone else that bothered me. I shook my head and pulled my braid over my shoulder, playing with the end.

He turned from the balcony and faced me. "She's really very sweet. You'll like her when you get to know her. Irwin too."

"When would that happen? Tomorrow? Friday? They're gone on Saturday. And I'm busy tomorrow and Saturday's a complete write off. You're going home." With a flick, my braid went flying and I folded my arms across my chest.

He sighed. "If it was important, I know I'd find a way to make it work."

"Like I said, don't bother. It doesn't matter. Whatever's bugging me, it'll go away." Eventually. As soon as I put some serious distance between us and bury myself into the new job.

"But I want to know what's eating at you." He pulled his hand from his pocket and lifted it ever so. It twitched like he wanted to touch me, and he was using all his power to keep from doing so, when it's all I wanted.

"Why? Why do you care?"

"Because it hurts that you suddenly shut me out."

Only because it affected him, not because I meant anything to him. The sting in my heart began to ache. I turned away from the pained expression he held and focused on the abstract art hanging on the wall beside the bed. "Just let it go. I know I'm going to have to." Some way, somehow. It's what I have to do.

"But we were having so much fun." There was a mild whine to his tone as he approached me.

"We were. But it was all a farce. You know it, and I now I know it."

Jon narrowed his gaze. "What was a farce?"

"All of it. Us. You. Me." I shifted my braid to come over my left shoulder and fiddled with the ends again. The motion was oddly soothing. "Look. I'm going to be honest with you. I'm not really Jessica." There, it was now out in the open. Just opened the proverbial door to make him leaving even easier.

"Do you have a twin?" He glanced around.

I went to the safe and unlocked it, retrieving my passport. Turning it to the right page, I showed him. "My real name is Tess. Tess Gallagher." I felt like it would be appropriate to extend my hand in greeting, but I kept it firmly by my side.

"Tess." The name rolled over his tongue a few times. Curiously, he took the passport and scanned it, sitting on the edge of the bed. "And this is your birthdate?"

"Yes."

He tapped a finger to his temple. "How cool is it that your birthday is the same day as Galileo?"

That was his reaction? I was floored he wasn't upset. He was more concerned about me sharing a birthday with some celebrity. "I'd say really cool, but I don't even know who that is. Is that a singer?" It sounded like a rap name.

He shook his head and a small smile started building on the edge of his lips. "He was an astronomer, the greatest of his time." Of course he was, and to Jon, this was common knowledge, but I had no idea. "He discovered the moons of Jupiter."

"Ah." I knew what Jupiter was. The planet with the red dot on it.

"Regardless, is this the only thing you've been untruthful about?" He handed me back my passport which I immediately locked back in the safe.

I stood beside the tub and peered into the few inches of water sitting in the bottom, cooling off. With the flick of switch, I set the tub to drain. "Yes. I'm not proud of it though."

Shaking his head, he said, "It's not that big a deal and I can understand a safety reason behind that." He rested his forearms on his legs. "Is that what's bothering you? You've been going around under a pseudonym?"

"No." My heart ached a little at what needed to be said. But damn it anyway. It was breaking and it was going to happen regardless of what I did to protect it. "What bothers me is that you're leaving on Saturday and that you live so far away. I didn't come to Mexico to find anything other than the best view and comfiest lounge chair, and instead I'm going home with heartache." I closed my eyes and covered my heart with my hand. As if that would help.

"Heartache?" His voice softened.

I opened my eyes to watch him sag further into the mattress.

"That's not what I wanted for you."

"Huh?"

"I came here at the behest of Irwin. I was getting into my head too much back home and was as he put it, insufferable. He practically begged me to come with them and spend the week messing around. That meeting some random chick from a place I'd never visit would help. He suggested a Central American."

My stomach flipped. "And that's where I came in."

"Yes."

"I was right." And I hated myself. All along I'd held out hope that I'd been wrong.

"Only if you think that's what ended up happening."

I lifted my focus off the floor and into his eyes.

He rose and started pacing. "That morning, I'd woken up from one of the worst nightmares I've had lately—that I'd gone completely blind before I had a chance to see everything I wanted to. And as I'd walked to the bathroom to wash my face, there was your note on the floor. Something about it was completely intriguing to me. I'm not stupid, I knew it wasn't intended for me, but still, I had to know who sent it."

"So, you came down to the beach hoping to find an easy score."

He stopped walking and hung his head. "Not my finest moment, but yeah. I stood at the end of the beach for a while, watching to see if anyone else was coming by but you were the only one there. Call me crazy, but after you snapped a picture of your wiggling toes with the ocean behind it, I just had to meet the T-bird." He gazed upon me. "What does that name mean?"

"I'm Tess, the T in T-bird. Camille started calling

me that back in high school. Our inside joke because she says I was born to fly. Anyway ..." I waved for him to continue.

"Right." He twisted his hands together. "The first time I saw you, you took my breath away. You were the most beautiful woman I'd ever seen."

An unattractive snort fell out of me. "Now I know you're lying."

"Nope." He resumed his pacing. "Just being there with you was a level of intoxication I didn't know existed. You were confident without being cocky about it, and the funny part is I don't think you even see that in yourself." His gaze roved up and down me. "When we strolled along the boardwalk that night and you actually took an interest in my stories, I was hooked. You looked at me differently than anyone else ever has. I don't know what it is, but being around you, I feel calm and collected, and I can be myself. You aren't afraid to be you. And believe me, that's refreshing."

"Well ..." I paused and debated saying anything else. "I'm not the adventure seeker you think I am."

"I gathered that you're not. Remember? I heard you scream behind me on the ATV and on your first zip line experience."

It was my time to hang my head in shame. "I

wanted to be that girl who does all that, so in a way, I am afraid to be me."

"Really?" He sat up straighter. "You did all those things, so there was no lying involved. That was all you. Unless you have a twin that you sent in your place."

That statement made a smile crack through my otherwise sullen expression. "There's no twin. Just me." Just boring ole Tess. "And trust me, the real me, she's not that exciting."

He shrugged. "I beg to differ. You've been pretty exciting here."

"Yeah, here. Back in the real world, not so much."

"Adulting sucks, doesn't it?" The deep pools of blue pierced through to my soul. "Back home, I'm no fun either. I work fourteen-hour days, six days a week. On the side of web development, I'm trying to develop software that will help me in the future. Want to talk about fun? That ain't it. Why do you think people take vacations?"

I sat on the bed opposite him. "You're not disappointed with me?"

An amused expression surfaced on his rugged face. "Truth be told, all this adventuring is a little exhausting." With that said, his smile deepened. "Sometimes you just need to have a day or two without plans while you're on vacation to escape your day-to-day."

"And there you go again, being all charming." It was heartbreaking that my time with him was so very limited. Why couldn't I have met him on the plane coming down here? Then I'd know he was from the same city. An across the city romance would work so much better than a two-country one. "And the worst part? All this ends on Saturday."

He sighed. "It almost ended today."

"But that's the thing. Something's happened over the course of the last four days. Something I'm not wanting to leave behind."

He inched himself closer to the edge of the bed. "I feel that too."

"You do? I thought I was just a distraction."

"Originally, yes." He stood and started pacing again. "All week long, I've been putting the brakes on as often as I can. That night at the boardwalk, I wanted to kiss you all night under the stars, but I asked myself if that's what you'd want."

Oh, I so did.

"And then the sunset sail. In all the world, there will never be a more romantic trip as that one. Never. I couldn't help myself, I needed to kiss you and hold you. It probably makes me sound girly to say this ... but I felt safe in your arms."

Sweet Jesus.

"Watching you on the beach during the ATV trip, well, that pushed me over. You were so free and fun and real. Believe me when I say you're the real deal. I couldn't hold back anymore. In that moment I knew I wasn't falling for you, I already had fallen for you, and it was the scariest damn feeling."

"I know that feeling all too well."

"You do?" He stood in front of me.

I rose and smiled. "It was happening to me too. That's why when you said it was all in fun, I was crushed. I've felt things for you that I'd never felt for my fiancé."

"You have a fiancé?" He stepped back and frowned.

"I *had* a fiancé. I kicked him out a few weeks ago. Honestly, at first it hurt so much to lose him, but now … he doesn't even hold a candle to you."

With an assessing eye, Jon studied me; his gaze roaming up and down my body with an intent focus on my face. A heartbeat and a breath later, he bridged the distance between us and cupped my cheek in his palm. "I'm so in love with you, Tess."

My heart bottomed out. "And you're leaving in three days. See the true problem?"

Chapter Sixteen

There we were, two grown adults with an ocean of heartache growing between us.

"I do see that problem." At least Jon had the good sense to finally understand the situation. It didn't matter if we had feelings for each other now, here. Come Saturday, he was flying to his home which was nowhere near mine. He was on the Atlantic side, and I was closer to the Pacific. I lived in Canada, he was American. "So, what are we to do?"

"Our options are limited. Very limited. We can either have one of two fairy tales: make the best of what we've got for the next couple of days and end it, or figure out how to transplant either one or both of us." My heart nearly snapped. "And we both know the practical answer is the first one."

He sighed, a soul-crushing sound that broke me.

Tears welled up and threatened to spill over the

dam, but I reined them back in. Crying now would solve nothing. What I needed was a solution. One that would last beyond Saturday, even if it was weak at best. Hell, I'd even settle for a fairy godmother and a flick of her magical wand.

"We could do a long-distance romance?"

"And that would work for the short-term only. Flying between countries every couple of months is a huge expense." As would moving to the US, which I didn't think would work given the whole needing a work visa and all that. It was impractical. Damn.

The tears fell out, single file at first and quickly turning into a river. There was no way to stop them. And suddenly I didn't want to try.

He held my hand and squeezed. "Honestly, I think the best thing we can do is to not think about Saturday."

"What? How?" It was three days away. It was at the forefront of my brain and came before every thought. How could I not think about it?

"We live for the next two days. Tomorrow we go on the turtle release and we enjoy every minute of it. Then you'll come as a guest to Irwin's wedding tomorrow night."

"Irwin's getting married? And I suppose that's at sunset?" It was starting to make a little sense why he was so focused on being back by a certain time.

"Is there another time to get married here?" He cocked an eyebrow, adding more sex appeal to him. Not that he needed it. "That's why I have all these abrupt get togethers. Him and Jacy threw it together at the last possible moment. Totally spontaneous on their part. They landed and thought it was a sweet idea and put it together. Aside from me, none of their friends are here. No family. Kind of crazy, really."

I couldn't even imagine trying to put that together in a few days. Power to them.

"But it's all taken care of. After they say I do tomorrow, I won't be seeing them. They're staying behind for another week while I need to jet home and attend to business." He brushed away my tears. "It can be just you and me all night long tomorrow and all day Friday."

"I like the sound of that." I pressed my tank top covered chest into him. The heat from his body warmed me when I didn't think I was cold.

"We can do anything you want." He trailed a finger over my cheek.

"Well, now I'm torn. Do we maximise our outings and try parasailing, or go snorkeling or even go to the nude beach on the island? Or do we spend our last minutes snuggling together knowing it's our last day?" It was crazy to think of it like that, but I couldn't wrap my head around knowing in two days, he'd be gone.

He brushed his lips across mine. "I think we can do it all. Or do nothing. As long as I'm with you, it will be the perfect ending to a perfect vacation." Tender fingers wiped under my eyes. "Don't be sad that it's ending, be happy that it's happened."

Poetic, and words I'd take with me to my grave. I nodded. "Okay."

"Now. I think we should dine on the best Italian food this resort has to offer. What do you say?"

I nodded, slowly. My stomach was in knots and I wasn't sure if I'd be able to eat anything.

"Slip into something more appropriate for supper, and I'll call and make the reservations."

It didn't dull the ache in my heart, but knowing that he felt the same way somehow made me feel better. At least on Saturday, I wouldn't be the only one upset.

It was unplanned, at least on my part, but waking up with Jon beside me was the best way to greet the morning.

"Good morning." He kissed the tip of my nose.

"Good morning." I raced to cover my breath.

"Stop. You're perfect."

I wanted to laugh, but his soft lips covered mine and I breathed him in. I could've kissed him for hours, but the alarm going off on my phone interrupted us. Over and over again. "We need to get ready."

I got dressed in a simple dress and ran a brush through my hair. Thankfully, it only had a hint of a wave which I blamed on the humidity.

"You're going to put sunscreen on, right? You know this release is out in full sun." He was stretched out across my bed, the thin white sheet hiding very little. And damn, it was sexy as hell.

"I have a hat." I wiggled over to the dresser and pulled out one of two floppy hats and pulled it on over my head.

Pulling on his shorts from last night, he walked over to the vanity and grabbed the bottle of sunscreen. "Turn around."

I slowly spun on the spot and pulled my hair off to the side. A shock of cold landed on my shoulder, followed by the warmth of his hand. He smeared the lotion over and rubbed it in. On my shoulders. Down my arms. Across the top of my back. As he finished rubbing the nape of my neck, his warm breath blew across it. I'd never been aroused by a sunscreen application before.

"That was nice."

"And now you're protected." He winked at me.

"You need to go and get changed. The bus leaves in twenty minutes and we haven't even had breakfast yet."

"It'll be ready. I had them prepare a take-away lunch. We can pick at that."

"You really thought of everything." I planted a kiss on his cheek.

Under his breath, he whispered, "Not everything."

I opened the door and jumped back when Camille stood there with her arm raised in the air.

She was about to smack on the door. Her eyes narrowed to slits and she shot multiple daggers at Jon and I. "What's going on?" Her voice was a sneer.

"We're going to rescue some turtles." I couldn't help but lock my fingers in with Jon's.

"Release them, actually," Jon corrected.

"Not together, you're not." Camille had her arms crossed over her chest, her right foot tapping the tiles beneath her.

"Yeah, we are." I marched right up to my best friend. "We chatted last night and we're both aware of what's going to happen. However, we don't care." I gazed back at Jon. He gave me a slight head nod. "We have two more days together and we intend on making it the best. Fill it with memories we'll never forget."

"Is that so?" Camille hasn't changed her stance.

"That's right."

"And neither of you care that you're way too involved."

I shook my head, as did Jon.

"Well …" There was no movement from her and I became worried she was about to snap. Camille the girl who flirts with everyone, and beds them just as fast, was giving me shit for sticking with one guy even if the end result would surely break me in two. I envied her and the way she kept her emotional distance from guys. "You know what I have to say to that, don't you?"

Yeah, good luck. Don't come running back to me. I stared her down.

Suddenly, she wrapped her arms around me and squeezed. "Well, get going then. You'll miss your ride."

"Thank you," I whispered into her ear.

"I hope you know what you're doing," she whispered back.

"I don't. And that's the best part." We broke away.

She stood beside Jon and the look on her face said it all. She gave him a hug. "And since you plan on breaking her heart, treat her like a lady should be treated until that moment comes. She's been through enough." She patted him on the shoulder and started walking away. "To love!"

Her voice echoed in the empty corridor.

"What are you going to do today?" I asked her.

"I don't know, I'll find someone." She giggled and waved goodbye to us.

"Well, that was ... unexpected." Jon stared at her with shock on his face.

"That's Camille for you." It was how it always was. Camille told you things straight up, but as fierce as she came across, she was a pussycat inside.

"Is she a drill sergeant back home?"

I laughed. "She's a kindergarten teacher."

"Shut up!" He stared into the hallway Camille had disappeared down and shook his head. It was sometimes hard to picture, but her students adored her, and the parents loved her as well.

Ten minutes later, we added our take-away lunch to my bag packed with sunscreen and water bottles. We joined the other excited tourists on the cramped and hot bus—aka a bigger minivan.

It would've been more comfortable if I'd ridden on Jon's lap, but that was something I wanted to save for later. In the meantime, we were packed in like sardines and I was grateful for the thin dress I wore, and the deodorant I'd put on. Someone in the van failed on that part.

The ride down the highway to the turtle sanctuary

was filled with endless chatter. One of the couples was from Vancouver, another from London, and a single lady with her daughter were from Florida. The older couple from London had done this once before and said it was the highlight of their vacation.

I glanced over to Jon. So far, he was the highlight, that and the magnificent sunset sail we went on. I doubted baby turtles could outdo the wonderful person snuggled into me.

The van took a hard left, and we veered down a bumpy road that indicated it was created on a dare. Full of potholes and bumps and ruts, my stomach started to sour at all the twists and turns. I pushed my nose to the vented back window, but the sewer-like smell wasn't any better.

Jon looked worse than I did, and an unhealthy shade of white settled over him. I dug through my bag, hoping to find some crackers or something. Not that I'd eat them at that moment, but maybe it would work on settling his stomach. His cheeks puffed out and instantly, I dumped the contents of the bag onto my lap and gave the thin plastic bag to him.

Trapped with nowhere to go, I turned my head as he emptied his stomach into the bag. My own stomach twisted with his retching sounds.

"Ew," the teenage girl who sat in front of him said

and inched closer to her mom.

The older man spoke up. "Driver, can we stop? A man just got sick."

"'Most there," he said as the van jumped over another bump.

"We're going to lose another," the mother said and quickly tapped me on the shoulder and gave me an empty lunch bag.

The bag crinkled in the tight grip of my hands, and I prayed I wouldn't have to use it. It was all a lie; I knew better. My stomach had been flipping and tossing before I even heard Jon's let go. Summoning up stomach tightening strength and begging for calmness to cover me, I closed my eyes and put my hand on the back of Jon's neck. I gave him a gentle squeeze to let him know I wasn't giving up on him. I felt bad that I was unable to look at him, and I tried desperately to drown out the noises that added to my internal misery. Hoping it would work, I pressed my nose out the vented part of the window and deeply inhaled. A fresh scent of salty ocean air was there. We were quickly approaching the ocean and the turtle sanctuary. Thank God.

We drove for a few more minutes, the road turning into a grassy stretch with fewer bumps and ruts, which eventually turned into hard packed sand. The van came to a stop and in the quickest order even seen, emptied out amazingly fast. Guess no one wanted to hear Jon puke again.

He stepped out, gripping his stomach and scampered over to the garbage barrel the driver pointed out. I was half a step behind him. There wasn't anything for my stomach to empty and instead I dry heaved twice before my body settled down. Yep, those were totally blamed on listening to Jon. Curse my weak stomach.

Using the wet napkin included with our lunch, I cleaned myself up and dabbed it across my forehead.

Jon did the same and gave his mouth a rinse with a swig of bottled water, spitting it into the barrel. He cocked an eyebrow at me. "Attractive, huh?"

"I'd tell you I've seen worse, but that would be a lie." I patted him on the shoulder. "This is what happens to me when I listen to someone puke."

He leaned against me under the blaring heat. Getting him out of the sun should be a priority. "You really are sensitive."

"Camille calls it empathetic. I call it pathetic."

It made a weak smile appear, and he took the offered drink of water, this time swallowing it. "Geezus, that was the roughest road. I'm not looking forward to that on the way home."

"We'll sit up front. Maybe it's not so bad up there."

"Let's hope." His hand slipped into mine and we started walking to the tented area where the group had disappeared.

It wasn't too far from the makeshift parking lot, but far enough in the sweltering temperature. The tented area wasn't really a tent at all. Upon closer inspection, it was a handmade creation crafted from logs with giant palm tree leaves overtop. Stepping under the roof, the temperature was a good ten degrees cooler and the reprieve was welcome. A light breeze blew and cooled my clammy, sweaty skin.

The seating area was big enough to comfortably hold fifteen picnic tables, with six guests at each. A BBQ sat at the furthest end where a shirtless man was grilling up something sweet and savoury. Even though I knew I shouldn't eat with my upset tummy, the smell was enticing all the same.

Our tour group sat on the one side, nearest a rickety building that should've been bull-dozed years ago. What we would call a snow fence surrounded a huge partition of sand in front of the ramshackle house, with several stakes in the ground. Each stake was roughly five feet apart and at a quick count, there were at least twenty of them.

The older gentleman from London handed both Jon

and I a cold bottle of water.

"Thanks," I said, taking the bottle and swallowing a few mouthfuls. A cool bubble of water slid down my throat and into my raw and empty stomach. Immediately though, I felt better. "Thanks," I said again as I sat down, giving a passing glance at Jon. "Are you going to sit?"

"Best I probably stand." He placed his hand on my shoulder.

I nudged his leg gently with my elbow. "Would you check out that view?"

Breathtaking wouldn't even describe it. The beach at our resort I'd give a nine out of ten, and the beach where we stopped on the ATV tour was most definitely a perfect ten. This put both of those to shame.

The white sand didn't just stretch out half a kilometre from us to the water, but it extended all along the coast as far as the eye could see. We were sheltered into a cove, as behind us were grassy hills, ironically very dry looking given our location. A tiny creek ran between the hills and dumped out onto the sand. We were too secluded under the palm trees, but the ocean in the distance was rolling and cresting, and practically pulled me over like a strong current.

A picture-perfect view indeed. If there was one place on earth I'd retire, it would be here. Rebuild that house and the road that led in, and it was ideal. The endless beach, the hot sun, the total privacy the entire place gave us. My retirement years could be sweet. Thinking about shacking up in my golden years, I glanced up at Jon. I'd bet the stars at night were as perfect as they could be, twinkling in their glory, and there'd be more in a small patch of sky than one could count. I was sure Jon would love it.

A serenity filled his previously taut face. Was it as relaxing to him? He, too, was taking it all in, scanning the horizon from left to right.

It dawned on me. He *was* taking it all in, likely memorizing every detail. My heart broke knowing in his golden years, he'd need to remember this view. There'd be no twinkling stars. No rolling surf. No white sandy beaches. It would all be darkness for him. Life was so unfair.

Chapter Seventeen

The turtle release coordinator, a tall man whose skin was as dark as tanned leather, went over the rules with us. It was fairly simple. As soon as the eggs hatched, we were to reach in with our gloved hand and grab one, putting it in our provided bowl. Then we could take all the pictures we wanted while we waited for the turtles to activate, which simply meant that they were moving around and able to right themselves if they ended up on their backs. That process took somewhere between forty-five minutes to an hour. When the turtles were fully activated, we'd take them down to the beach and release them.

It sounded simple enough.

However, the eggs hadn't hatched yet, so the cook continued barbecuing and served us up roasted mango and pork on a skewer. Since my stomach was feeling better, I had one and it was beyond tasty. Sweet and salty were the perfect combo. Jon refused, but I didn't blame him. He was still looking a little unhealthy but at least he was drinking some water and staying hydrated.

He sat on the bench. "Is it okay if I give you a massage?" He nodded and placed his forearms on the table, rolling his shoulders forward.

His shirt was soft, and I gently kneaded my fingers through the collar, digging my thumbs into the base of his neck. He groaned slightly as I rubbed the knot on his spine. Keeping firm pressure, I continued to dig into his strong shoulders and back. Beneath my fingers, he began to relax, and in feeling that, it released tension from me, and I started feeling better as well.

It was the best-case scenario. I pushed up against his back and stroked my hands around his neck and over his chest. Palms flat, I ran them over his pecs, trying to keep it as unsexy as possible. I failed. Just touching him was firing up my internal thermometer, and there was only one way to extinguish those flames.

He pulled me into his lap, and without a care in the world, kissed me, knocking my floppy hat onto the sand. "Damn, Tess, do you know what that does to me?"

My mind squealed in hearing him address me by my real name. If I'd known it'd sound that sexy rolling off his tongue, I would've said it originally. "I'd be interested in finding out," I smiled. It was great seeing him returning to himself.

One by one, our tour group was called over to one of the stakes where a deep, dark hole was visible, and each came back with a red bucket and a baby turtle in it.

I kissed him quickly. "We're up. Do you have your name picked out?"

The guide suggested that we have names ready, and I'd heard some of our travellers call out their names: Leonardo, Michelangelo, and other Ninja Turtle names, along with some truly unique monikers such as Dixie and Myrtle.

"One will come to me," he said, walking hand in hand with me through the hot sand over to the pit in the ground.

I knelt onto the sand, fearing the heat from the sand would leave burn marks on my shins.

The guide gave me a pair of gloves. "You're going to reach down into the hole and grab a turtle."

I must've missed something. I thought he, as in the coordinator, was going to grab one and place it onto our hands and *we* place it into the bucket. Didn't think I'd have to reach into that hole. Who knew what was in there?

"Go ahead," Jon said, gloving up.

"What's the name?" The guide pointed to the hole.

The only name to come to me was the surfer turtle from *Finding Nemo*. A laugh rippled through me as I giggled out, "Crush," and stuck my hand into the dark hole. Turtles moved all around, bumping against my hand. *It's not big bugs*. With a little trepidation, I gently clutched one and pulled it out.

"Welcome, Crush." He handed me a bucket and looked at Jon.

"What was the name of Crush's kid?"

I scrunched up my face, trying to remember. It had been a while since I'd watched it last. "Squirtle?"

"That's a Pokemon, but you know what, that works too." A moment later he pulled out his Olive Ridley turtle.

"Welcome, Squirtle."

"Oh my gosh," Jon whispered, as he set his turtle into the bucket I'd held onto firmly. The two siblings raced for each other like it had been years since they'd seen each other and not a few seconds. It was sweet.

We rose and headed back under the cover of the tent where we sat and stared at our baby turtles.

"They're so cute." Jon kept his hand in the bucket, allowing the turtle babies to bump against it.

Seriously, they were adorable. My turtle had three distinct white markings on its back with broad dark etchings, and Jon's three white markings were much wider. They shuffled around their bucket, pushing the other out of the way or climbing up on top of the other's shell. They were unsuccessful in escaping the high walled sides of their temporary home. I couldn't peel my eyes away from them.

We took turns holding our turtles in the palm of our hands and snapping pictures. While we waited for them to 'activate' as the guide said, I tried my best to not handle them so much. They were wild creatures after all, but I couldn't stop from touching and found myself running my finger along the ridges on the hardening shell.

I leaned against Jon, who hadn't stopped staring at his turtle either. "Look at Squirtle. He's so helpful, pushing his big brother back onto his fins." Indeed, it was oddly endearing watching the one baby turtle use his nose to get under the shell of the other and assist.

"Perhaps, despite the odds, they're going to make it." Those deep blue eyes of his connected with mine.

My heart swelled at the double meaning. "I hope so."

After the last couple hatchlings were ready to go, our guide led us out to the ocean and stopped about twenty feet from where the waves lazily lapped against the sand.

With a walking stick, he drew a line in the sand as a starting point. He demanded that without touching the turtles, who had been manhandled enough apparently, we tip the buckets and let the turtles go. By the position of the sun in the sky, they'd know to instinctually follow it to the ocean.

I kneeled on the cool, damp sand beside Jon, and hand in hand, we released our babies out of their buckets. "Go, Crush."

"Go, Squirtle."

We took a dozen more photos. My turtle made a mad dash for the water, little fin marks creating a pattern in the sand. Jon's turtle was a little confused and started heading the other way.

"Don't touch." The guide came over as Jon went to intercept. "He'll figure it out. He needs to if he's going to make it out there." He pointed his walking stick towards the rolling waves.

My gaze darted between Crush, who was nearing the receding edge of the wave, and Squirtle, who looked as if he was trying to make it back to the shelter. Eventually, he turned around and raced to catch up with his siblings.

All along the beach were the fin markings of nearly seventy babies as they inched their way to their new homes. Waves splashed against the sand, washing the turtles out to sea. Some were still making their way closer to the water, like Crush, and there were those who enjoyed taking in the scenery. Jon had a turtle that matched his personality; he was content to take in his surroundings too.

We rested on the edge of the ocean, head to head, watching out over the waves, wondering if our turtles would survive. The odds weren't great according to the guide, but by protecting them until they hatched, we'd already given them a better head start. Watching the turtles, I couldn't help but make parallels to Jon and me.

Our odds weren't great either. Like a sea turtle out in the ocean, the chances were about twenty-five percent that they'd make it to a year old. Similar, I thought, to a long-distance relationship. So many other things to thwart the survival, and only the strongest will make it. Our biggest hurdle lay only a couple days ahead of us ... Saturday. The clock was ticking.

Chapter Eighteen

Our van pulled up to the entrance of the hotel and being in the front, we got to escape the un-air-conditioned space first.

We walked to the elevators, feeling much better on the return trip than we had fared going to the sanctuary.

Jon's hand rested on my hip. "I need to do a few things, but I'll meet you on the beach in half an hour? You don't need to wear anything fancy."

"I'll be there." I wrapped my arm through his and leaned against him as the elevator lifted us higher.

"You know what, on second thought, I want to pick you up and escort you down to the venue. Can you be ready in fifteen?" He nuzzled the side of my neck, leaving little kisses in the hollow.

"You keep kissing me like that, and you'll be late and miss this wedding." I closed my eyes, allowing the sensations to tremor in my core.

The elevator chimed and the doors opened, stopping the fun we were having.

"My floor," he said, blowing a kiss in my direction as he stepped into the foyer.

"Fifteen minutes."

"Maybe less." The doors closed and a moment later, opened on my floor. I sped to my room and dashed around wondering what I was going to change into and how to do my hair. My dress options were exceptionally limited. After all, I'd expected a week on a lounge chair and had packed accordingly. Bathing suits I had in reserve but nice dresses? I only had two, and I'd worn both already.

The halter-top dress with the blue sash was my best bet even though it was white. Wasn't that a faux pas? But it was also a beach wedding, so maybe regular rules didn't apply? I hung the dress in the back of the shower to steam it out while I quickly hopped in and washed off the sunscreen and sand residue, giving my legs a quick shave.

I'd barely finished dusting my face with setting powder and pulled the dress over my head when a knock came on my door. I yanked it open, breathless at the speed in which I'd gotten ready, to the most adorable man I'd ever given my heart.

"Hey, handsome." His hair was slicked back, and

he wore a light blue button-down with white shorts that somehow made his eyes sparkle a lighter shade. Guess my dress wouldn't be so out of place. His gaze roved up and down my body.

"Wow, you look amazing."

A slight warmth flooded my cheeks and chest, but I was getting a bit of a tan, so hopefully the blush wasn't as noticeable. "Thanks." I held up two pair of shoes. "Which ones are more appropriate for the wedding?"

"It's right on the beach, so those, since you'll be barefooted."

I tossed the strappy sandals into the closet and slipped the nicer looking flip flops onto my feet. Phone in hand, I linked my arm through his, and we headed toward the beach.

The ambient lighting around the pool decks was coming on, although the sun had yet to set. All the way to the beach we were greeted by a heavenly floral scent, and a perfectly warm breeze. Irwin was going to have the most magical wedding.

As we descended upon the cool sand, I removed my shoes and Jon set them off to the side. "The beach is reserved for the next hour. You won't have to carry your shoes."

An archway had been erected a few feet away, and

tables with Bluetooth speakers were set up around the area. A dozen white chairs with beige organza bows faced toward the setting sun. Considering how this was essentially tossed together, I was more than a little surprised at how many seats were available. No family or friends were expected.

"You'll have a seat here, as I'll be over there, helping Irwin."

I turned my head to look where he'd pointed, and at the far end of the beach stood Irwin.

Jon placed a sweet kiss upon my lips. "I need to go to him, but I promise I'll be back. Save a dance for me?"

"I'll save all my dances for you." I kissed him once more for good measure and held on to his hand as long as I could before he broke away.

I took in the surrounding atmosphere. Toes squishing into the sand, the rolling ocean, the sun lowering itself closer to the horizon, the soft Enya-like music playing from the speakers. It was so relaxing, and I could honestly see myself surrounded by it 24/7 and never grow old of it. Guess that's why this was paradise for many.

My gaze lingered on the stunning man who'd unbuttoned his top button and gave his hair a bit of a fluff. He truly looked beach wedding ready, and I found myself wondering how I'd gotten so lucky. How the stars had intervened, and I'd sent the right note under the wrong door. Was it fate? I wasn't sure. But it was the best damn vacation I'd ever had. I highly doubted any in the future would compare.

Resort guests made their way through the sand and took a seat. I kept my laughter at the absurdity to myself. Who watches a stranger's wedding from the best seats in the house? Maybe from up on the boardwalk, but right down on the beach? It was definitely strange.

The music changed tempo, and Irwin and Jon ambled over to the arch. I was a little surprised at the true ready-to-jump-into-the-water beachwear Irwin wore, but I suppose it was his wedding, his choice. A justice of the peace stood behind, his back to the lowering sun. All five heads turned as the bride-to-be waltzed towards her betrothed. The petite woman strode down the stairs and onto the sand wearing a white see-through cover-up overtop a white bikini, holding a single white rose. She sauntered over to Jon and gave him a kiss on his cheek as Jon turned his head at the last second, and then linked fingers with Irwin.

After they exchanged vows, they both went for a swim. In a weird way, it reminded me of a baptism, but yet it wasn't. Jacy managed to keep everything above her shoulders dry after she removed her cover up and took the plunge with Irwin. The whole wedding ranked up there as one of the most unique I'd witnessed.

Someone yelled, "Party time!" and bolted to the boardwalk behind us, following it to the Oyster Bar at the far end.

"Just wait," Jon pulled me close. "I want you to officially meet my friends."

Irwin, whom I'd met on my first day, carried his new bride out of the water and onto the beach. Both made their way over to us.

"Jacy, Irwin, I'd love you to meet Tess."

Irwin shook my hand. "Hey."

Jacy roved her gaze over me and I braced myself, unsure of what to expect. Suddenly, she wrapped her arms around me in a hug. "So pleased to meet you. I've heard all about you." She pulled back and beamed, true sincerity crossing her petite face.

I smiled back at her.

"C'mon. There's a party over there starting without us. Let's go!" She grabbed Irwin's hand and with barely a grunt, he lifted and swung her up into his arms. Their giggles were infectious.

Jon grabbed my hand and we climbed up the stairs, intent on joining the other wedding guests.

"Romantic wedding, wasn't it?" Jon asked when

we were out of earshot of the bride and groom.

I raised my brow. "I don't know if I'd call it romantic, it was different. But as long as they're happy, that's all that truly matters."

"Not how you'd do it?" Jon slowed his pace.

"It wasn't my wedding, so it's not important."

"But if you could plan yours?"

"Well, that's a loaded question."

We stopped at our spot in the alcove of the boardwalk. Jon sat down, and I snuggled in beside him. He lifted my legs over his and tenderly stroked my calves.

"How's it loaded?"

"Because, I'm not getting married at this exact moment."

"But if you were?"

I sighed and considered my options. "Going based on where I am in my life right now, and using only that as a marker for how I'd plan my future wedding …" I drifted my gaze away from Jon's and out onto the ocean. "I suppose I'd have a beach wedding, at sunset too. A resort like this is nice because all the food and drinks would be included, and I wouldn't have to consider menu choices. As for attire, something simple like what I'm wearing now would be enough, although I'd do more with my hair. I'd want it to look elegant."

He brushed away the strands that breezed into my face. "Did you and your fiancé consider a beach wedding?"

I shook my head, locking my focus back on the man of the moment. "I'm pretty sure he only asked me because he'd run out of available options. Looking back, I can see we weren't suited for each other. He's probably much happier with the girl he's with now."

Jon stroked the side of my face. "Had you set a date?"

"No, and we really hadn't even discussed the possibility of marriage. He popped the question in the most unromantic way. We were sitting in his truck and out of the blue he handed me a ring that looked like it came from the dollar store and said, 'If you know what this is and you put it on, then I guess we'll do the deed.' I mean, there was, like, zero romance behind it." I hung my head. "I'm not sure why I thought he hung the moon."

"Sounds like you've done some growing since you split up."

"Growing up?" I wiggled my hand. "Not sure about that, but I've definitely done some hard-core thinking. My world used to revolve around him and his needs ..."

"And in the real world, there should be some

compromising." His fingertips trailed down my neck and over my shoulder. "And for the love of God, there needs to be romance. Especially in a proposal."

"Romance doesn't hurt, that's for sure." I ran my hands up his strong arms and linked them behind his neck.

"Every woman needs to be treated like a lady. You remember what I said about Andromeda?"

I racked my brain, remembering the story but not all of the details. "I'm not chained to a rock. And my mother certainly didn't sacrifice me."

"Maybe you weren't literally tied to a rock, but I think metaphorically you were."

I gazed into his eyes, wondering if he was seeing into the depths of my soul through mine. "And you set me free?" It came out as a whisper. He didn't need to answer, I already knew the response to that. In several ways, he had set me free. I pressed my lips into him with an intensity and an urge for more.

His hands found the small of my back, and he pulled me closer as I tightened my grip around him. While the waves crashed against the rocks below us and soft music played from the Oyster Bar down the boardwalk, I surrendered my heart to Jon, knowing that after the week finished up, there'd be no more.

"I could do this all night," Jon said, breathless

between kisses.

"Me too."

"But I need to make an appearance for supper."

I sighed and agreed.

"After dinner, you're all mine."

"Promise?" I couldn't wait to strip him out of his shirt and run my hands over his chest while kissing every square inch of his magnificent body. As it was, I threaded my fingers through his hair, pressing kisses along the edge of his jaw and up over to his ear.

He held my hands tightly and set them in my lap. "You need to stop." The pleading in his eyes fell to his lap. "I need a moment to … umm … settle down."

Oh. OH! After a few minutes of me resting my head on his shoulder with his arms draped around me, he was ready to go. But I could've stayed like that all night. It was comforting and peaceful, and I needed to get as much as I could because Saturday was quickly approaching.

Chapter Nineteen

Camille and Seth, a boy toy she'd been with on Thursday, sat on the lounge chairs beside Jon and I. Seth went for a dive in the pool, showing off his dark, sleek body, and Jon went to order some poolside food.

It was the first time I'd had any privacy with Camille all morning.

"One would almost think that Seth was serious. Two days in a row."

She closed her eyes and rolled onto her back. "He's delicious. And let me tell you, all that mango and pineapple he eats has a positive effect."

"On what?"

"Let me repeat—he's delicious." Her eyebrows wiggled above her sunglasses.

Oh, I got it.

"Feed Jon some fruit and you'll see."

"Maybe I already—you know what, we're not

having this conversation." Some things were just not to be discussed.

"You know, I debated all morning telling you something and thought better of it, but I'm going to tell you anyways." She twisted on to her side and readjusted her bikini top. "I saw you last night."

Okay, big deal. We didn't do anything embarrassing. After dinner, we'd walked back to our spot along the edge of the ocean on the boardwalk and hung out.

"You were dancing."

We'd done that for a while. "So what?" The music from the Oyster Bar was just at the right level, and we'd had the alcove all to ourselves. The setting was too perfect to abandon, and although we'd known we'd end up back at my room, we'd wanted to spend time under the stars.

"I'm going to level with you. Whatever is going on between you and Jon, let me tell you something, it's the real thing."

"What?" I felt like I needed to throw that out there. It was becoming painfully obvious to me that it was the real thing too, but I needed to find a way to soften the upcoming hurt. I had twenty-four hours left with this wonderful man. After that, he was going home to Maine, and I was going back to winter. It didn't matter if we felt perfect for the other. Our future ended tomorrow when he boarded the shuttle bus to the airport. My track record with long-distance relationships was like oil and vinegar—it just didn't mix.

"Tess, I've known you for what? Twenty years? I've seen you in many relationships. None of them could even hold a candle to this. You two go together like …"

"Impending heartache."

"Well, that's going to happen tomorrow and I'm sorry I won't be around to comfort you after he abandons you."

Where she could only get the one-week trip due to needing to be back at school fresh as a daisy on Monday morning, I wasn't due to start the new job for another week. After Jon and Camille left, I still had three long days on my own.

"To be honest, I'm a little heartbroken for the both of you. You're a match made in the tropics." She flopped onto her back and stretched out her long, thin body.

"What about you? And Trey?"

"I'm going home, and I'm going to dump his sorry ass. If anything, this week has been an education. I don't need him to make me happy. Of all these guys I've been with this week, Seth has been the most normal, and even he's unattainable in the long run. Besides, I'm not missing

Trey. Doesn't that say something?"

I nodded. After being gone almost a week from someone, a part of you should be missing them, and if you're not? Well, then it isn't meant to be. "Jon's only been gone for five minutes, and I miss him."

"You're also a little infatuated with him too, so I'd blame the longing on that. However, did you ever miss Filipe when you were together?"

I shrugged. At first, our time apart was hard, but then it got easier, like a habit. Thinking back on it now, even when we lived together, a part of me looked forward to the nights where he was going to be gone.

"I'm not a relationship expert in the least."

I chuckled at how right she was.

"But I think you weren't in love with Filipe. Not really. You were in love with the idea of being in love with Filipe." She lifted her hand and gazed at me. "Do you agree or disagree?"

"Then why was I so upset when I had to kick him out?"

"Because it wasn't the fairy tale you'd hoped for. And truly, Filipe was no Prince Charming. When you needed to dispose of the garbage, it wasn't heartbreak over Filipe, it was heartbreak over the loss of the idea of growing old with someone you trusted."

Well, damn. Maybe it *was* the notion I was upset with. But that wasn't going to happen now while I could max out all the pleasure. I tossed my things into my day bag and grabbed all of Jon's things as well.

"Where you going?"

"I'm going to find my Perseus and live out the rest of my fairy tale."

"Your what?"

Without another word, I tore away from Camille and searched out the bar, finally finding Jon at the end of the line for food. "Put the tray down, we're going."

"We are?" An inquisitive expression crossed his face.

I was taking the bull by the horns. "Yep. We're going to take that boat over to the island and you and I are going to spend our final day together basking in the sun."

"We were doing that." He tipped his head over to where our chairs sat beside the pool.

"Alone."

He dropped the tray and took a hold of the bag. "Let's go."

After a short walk to the marina, we caught the water taxi and Jon fastened on his life jacket. The driver, since we were the only passengers, dropped us off at a private beach on the south end of the island.

"Last boat leaves the island at six. You go dere," he pointed to the thatched hut along a strip of beach, "and we bring you back." He motored along the coast. "Da topless beach is around the rocky edge, over dere." Pulling into a sandy area, he cut the engine to the boat and we hopped out, plunging into the cool, shallow water.

"Really?" Jon's smile matched mine. "That's something I've never done."

"Perfect." I held his hand as we sloshed our way through the knee-deep water and up to the vacated beach. "I want you to go home a love-starved man who won't be able to look at another woman without seeing me."

"Too late." He spun me around, and the boat fired up its motor and zoomed away from us. "It's already going to happen." He kissed me and my lips parted, giving him unrestricted access.

"Ever made love on a beach?"

He shook his head. "But not until you've sunscreened up first."

"What's with you and the sunscreen?" I joked as we shuffled up the beach towards a shadowed area.

"Remember how I mentioned Amy?"

The woman he dated and dumped because she wanted a future with him, and he didn't. I nodded.

"She wasn't truthful with me. Yes, she wanted me to see her in a wedding dress, but it wasn't just because my eyesight was going downhill. She'd kept her skin cancer diagnosis from me."

I covered my mouth. "And you dumped her."

"Not knowing, but still, yeah. I found out a couple of months later. I tried to get back together with her and make things right, but the damage had been done."

"Did she …?" I couldn't even bring myself to say the word.

"Die? No. Last I heard, she's recovered nicely. Complete remission."

"That's a relief."

"It is. However, I'm a big promoter of slathering on protection. It never hurts to be safe." He winked.

"Well, then there'll be no lovemaking on the beach. I have nothing for you." I hadn't had the foresight to bring any condoms with me on either the whole wild trip or this last-minute hop-in-a-boat-and-go-to-the-island trip.

"I do. Besides, there are other things we can do …" His words trailed off as he wrapped his arms around my waist and pushed himself against me. "But I look forward to rubbing sunscreen all over your body first."

We unrolled the towels we'd brought, and I wiggled out of my shorts, letting my gaze run up and down his amazing body that I could no longer wait to straddle and ride.

"Don't you feel exposed here?" Jon looked a tad uncomfortable, glancing over my shoulder.

Across the bay, the tower of our resort stood tall, but the people walking around were hard to make out unless you squinted. We were tucked into a jut of rocks, on smooth, hot sand. Based on our position, it wouldn't be long before the sun was behind the tip of the island and this area would be blanketed in shade. It was perfectly private. No one should be able to see us in the shade.

I reached behind my back and unhooked my top, letting it fall onto the sand. "Would you mind sunscreening me up?" I batted my eyelashes at him.

And that began one of the most amazing moments of my life. He made sure every inch of my body was protected from the sun, either with sunscreen or by his body. In turn, I made sure he was well-protected also. When we were spent and sweaty from the all the lovemaking, it was perfectly natural to lie in the shade, my nude body pressed into his, with my head on his chest listening to his rhythmic breathing.

"I love you," I whispered, moving my hand over his heart.

I'd found my sanctity, three thousand miles away

from where I thought it was. Where the waves crashed against the rocks, and in the distance, birds cawed and chirped. And the man who'd stolen my heart, laid with his own heart beating beneath the palm of my hand. They were beating in time to the other.

His muscles contracted a touch, and he woke up.

"Are you enjoying your afternoon?" I twirled my fingers over his chest, making invisible designs.

"It was magical." He kissed my forehead and squeezed my hip his hand rested upon. "I could go again."

"It'll have to be quick. The shadows are getting longer and the last boat leaves at six."

"What happens if we don't make it over? Do you think they drive around the island and double-check no one's here?"

I didn't know. But it wasn't an idea I wanted to entertain either. Safety was across the bay. We had no food or bottled water, having finished it off earlier. Deep, guttural growls were coming from my stomach.

"Come on, we'll go." He rolled himself up into a sitting position. "I can tell that you're not wild about staying."

Bags packed, we walked to the shoreline and splashed through knee-deep water around an outcropping of rocks which separated us from the family friendly zone where the water taxis awaited.

We approached the boat, already loaded with five passengers, and climbed aboard. Jon selected the middle seat, and held on tight. I took the only available seat in the bow and smiled. There was something amazing with the salty air blowing into my face that was setting me free. I inhaled huge lungfuls and savoured the smell.

Our walk back from the marina included us passing by the Oyster Bar, a restaurant destination that had become a favourite for us.

"Hola," our hostess greeted us. "Name?"

"We don't have a reservation, but we're wondering if you can get us in?" Jon asked in a sweet voice that anyone would've had a hard time saying no to.

She glanced around at the nearly empty place and searched her reservation schedule in front of her. Nodding, she grabbed two menus.

Hands locked together, we followed her to a table overtop the ocean. We were above the water level by a dozen feet at least, and far enough out that we wouldn't hear the water kiss the rocks, but also distanced away from the other patrons that it felt private.

"This is perfect, thanks," Jon said, holding out my chair.

I sat and covered my lap with my linen napkin.

The hostess handed us our menus and excused herself.

Jon pushed his menu off to the side. It was likely he was going to order the same thing he always did, the seafood ceviche.

I preferred something a little tamer and knew ahead of time I'd be ordering the seafood pasta. I joined him in closing up my menu.

He reached for my hands and tenderly caressed his thumb over my knuckles. "Why does tonight feel like the last night on the *Titanic*?"

I wanted to answer, *because we're doomed*, but thought better of it. "I don't know. They didn't know it was coming, but we do."

"I want to be like *Groundhog Day* and relive this day over and over."

A weak smile blossomed out of my lips. "Me too."

"I know we said we wouldn't talk about it and just take these final hours as they came, but I want to know what happens to us after tomorrow." For the first time all day, there was tension in his shoulders and stress around his eyes.

I shrugged as I didn't know. I didn't have the foggiest idea. "There's just too many variants to a possible long-distance relationship."

"We can't break up," his voice cracked just enough to make one on my heart. "Because the thought of you seeing someone else doesn't sit well with me."

I dropped my gaze and stared at our hands. The hurt on his face was much too hard to handle. "I feel the same. But what are we going to do? You can't just up and move. I just can't up and move. There'd be so much paperwork and visas needed for us to work in the other's country." My eyes watered up and I closed them and tucked my chin down to avoid him seeing. "And visiting? We'd have to meet in the US because, surprisingly, it's cheaper for me to fly into the US then it is to fly within my own country. But how often would we meet?"

"Whatever it takes. I want to see you as often as it's possible."

"And I want that too." Painful bubbles of hurt swirled in my gut. "But I'm the kind of girl who needs the physical contact all the time when I'm with someone. The distance between us will be too painful, and the soul-crushing need to feel you in my arms is heartbreaking. There's just no way this can work out for either of us." It became hard to swallow, and even harder to breathe.

He switched chairs and sat beside me, wrapping his arm around me. And it confused me since I both wanted to be held in his arms, and I also knew I needed some distance. My heart won out and I rested my forehead on his shoulder, feeling his hands rub the small of my back. "We'll get it figured out. I promise."

We wouldn't. It was impossible.

He pulled back and tipped my chin up. "We're Perseus and Andromeda. This is our sea monster, and we'll conquer it." His voice cracked again, and his eyes shone brighter in the reflection of the lights. "We have to."

Oh, my stars, how I wanted to believe him.

Our waiter came by and faced us both. I could only imagine the scene he gazed down upon.

I turned to Jon, trying to blink away my misery. "Can I order?"

"Yeah, sure."

To the waiter, I asked, "If we order this, can we get it to go?"

"Of course, even with a view like this?"

Indeed. The sun was getting ready for another beautiful Mexican sunset, and with the few lingering clouds, it promised to be quite the show. The air temperature was perfect to leave my shoulders exposed without need of anything to cover them, and the breeze coming off the ocean was warm.

"Yes, it is rather enchanting," I told the waiter, "but I have something else in mind." I tapped to what we'd both eat, including dessert.

The waiter took off.

"Now I'm curious, what you have in mind?" Jon once again wrapped his arms around me.

"You'll see. I want tonight to be a night to remember."

"I'm not sure how you'll top this amazing week. Every day with you has been one to remember." His lips found mine, and I melted into him.

Tomorrow night was going to be painful.

Chapter Twenty

With a bag full of food, cutlery, and napkins, we left the Oyster Bar behind. Our last visit. Hand in hand walking down the boardwalk, I turned and took it in, trying to memorize the way the lights from the railing bounced off the waves below. How in just the right spot, the spray rose up after a larger waved crashed against the rocks beneath. My sound machine at home was all a lie—this was the real deal and could never be duplicated.

His hand stayed firmly entwined with mine, and taking in the colours the setting sun splashed against the tower, we continued our walk along the boardwalk.

I took the lead as we approached the beach and kicked off my shoes, leading us up a sharp right-hand turn after four stairs.

I don't know how I'd missed it before, but I had noticed it when we motored over from the island. There was a smaller hidden beach tucked off to the side of the resort, with two cabanas on it. Behind the gauzy white linen roof were towering bushes and small trees, which was why I hadn't discovered them from the infinity pool nor my room. However, the view in front of the cabanas was completely unobstructed.

I kept my head turned away as we tiptoed over to the farthest cabana, as a couple were making out in the first one. The male party drew the beige canvas curtain across that separated the two cabanas, providing them with some privacy, even though their hotel room was the best spot for that.

"You can't beat this view, eh?" I hopped onto the queen-sized mattress and crossed my legs while pulling out our still-steaming supper. Fried fish smells circled all around us.

Jon sat on the edge of the cabana, left leg dangling over the edge, and opened up his box of food. "This is pretty nice. You have twilight," he arched his hand across the sky, "the crickets chirping, and hot food with an ocean sprawling out in front of us. But the best part is I'm sitting with the prettiest lady ever. Truly, you can't beat this at all." He stabbed his food with his fork and lifted it up to me. "Try it."

I hesitated, but cautiously opened my mouth, wrapping my lips seductively around the prongs of the fork. Slowly and methodically, I pulled back and chewed a bite of calamari.

"Only you could make eating sexy." His smile was wide and even in the darkening skies, I could see his eyes dancing.

"Oh, I'm only getting warmed up," I winked while I whispered, and copying his move, twirled some of my pasta onto my fork and presented it to him.

His bite came complete with a slow gripping of my right thigh with his left hand. With a ghost of a touch, he trailed his hand up toward my hip and let it linger as he opened his mouth in a slow, sensual way, his tongue flicking against the pasta.

And fuck me, I was ready to cream my bikini bottoms right there. I was pretty sure a groan slipped out of me too.

"Now now, we'll have time for that later."

We took turns sharing food and preparing for a hard workout. Each touch was a turn on, each look was captivating, and each smile was enough to make me lose control. Food done, we gathered up our garbage and hung the bag from one of the hooks on the edge of the cabana.

"Is my galaxy visible?" I asked in the quietest of tones, sliding to the edge of the mattress and gazing up into a sky filled with bright dots of light that meant absolutely nothing to me.

Jon craned his neck. "Let me see." He stared at the sky and mumbled directions. There were probably so many it would be hard to tell. "We're seeing it all wrong." He stood in the sand and turned around.

I hopped off and came to stand in front of him. He wrapped his arms around me, and I melted into his chest.

"There she is," he pointed to the sky. It didn't help. Lifting his hand, he made a line across the inky curtains of twinkling stars. "And Perseus is right behind her."

"Just like we are now." I pushed my hands behind me and ran my hands down his hips. Using all my restraint, I held him tightly, wanting and needing so much more than I had a right to.

Desire, firm and strong, responded to my touch and pushed into my ass. His breath was warm as he nipped at my ear.

I led him back to the cabana, where he crawled into the centre of the mattress. Moving slowly, I slid over to him and straddled him as I ran my fingers through his thick hair and he kissed down my neck. "Tell me another story about love in the stars." I tipped my head back when he found the sweet hollow in my collarbone.

"The best story is the one I've already told you." His lips kissed up my chin and landed firmly on my lips.

I parted them and allowed him to enter, all velvet and hot, dancing and mingling together. Pressure grew underneath me, and I couldn't wait to feel him inside me again. One of my hands reached around to his back and pulled him closer, while the other traced a path down to his heart. I pressed my palm against the racing beat, feeling it increase as I probed the depths of his mouth with my tongue.

"Take me."

He pulled back, cool air rushing into the space between us. "Here?"

"Yeah, no one will know." I wiggled my hips over him. We were already perfectly lined up. I could quickly remove my shorts and slip my bottoms off to the side, and just give his pants a little unzip ...

"There's another couple right beside us."

"Haven't you ever been to a make out point?"

"We're not crazy teenagers." There was a hint of curiosity though on the tip of his tongue.

"No, but we could be." I grabbed his hand and placed it above my own pounding heart. The fact that my breast was there was a bonus.

He studied my face, his hand resting against the small of my back and walked his fingers over to the other side of my waist and pulled me tight. "For you, I'll do it."

"I don't want you to feel apprehensive. We can go upstairs and make love up there."

Lips full of lust and love claimed me. "I love it when you say things like that."

"I love that you love me." For so many reasons that would be hard to put into words.

"I really do, Tess." He pressed his hips into mine.

I slithered out of my shorts and tucked them behind Jon's back. The unmistakeable crinkle of a wrapper opening permeated the air, and I wanted to hush it. Jon rolled it on, and with a little effort, I slid my bikini bottoms off to one side and pulled myself closer.

My arms tangled around him and through his hair, touching and caressing and putting it all into the deepest recesses of my memory. In a heartbeat, he repositioned me and we were one, connecting on a physical level that surpassed our previous couplings. There was an urge, a desire, a need we had to fulfill under the blanket of stars in the inky darkness beside the ocean. We were fast and furious, and full of satisfaction as he exploded into me with a thrust that could've launched me straight to Andromeda.

I cupped his face between my hands and breathed in his sweet, spent scent. "I love you, Jon." Before the tears could be seen, I nuzzled against his neck and held him securely. It felt like my life depended on it.

He didn't pull away. Rather, his embrace tightened, holding me as close as he could against his quivering chest. A heart pounded intensely, but I was at a loss as to whose it was.

Our breaths calmed, and my flow of tears stemmed, we separated briefly.

After readjusting, and disposing our personal garbage, I snuggled against him, my shoulder in his armpit and my head on his chest. It felt as natural as breathing to lie like that.

"I could get lost in this moment forever …" The words from Aerosmith's song floated in my heart and out through my mouth.

"I could spend my life in this sweet surrender," Jon added.

"You messed it up." But I was still smiling, the lyrics sang in the distance as if they were made for us.

A scratching sound made me jump and I bolted straight up on the mattress. I was still in the cabana, and the towel that had been covering me up flew to my feet.

A gardener tipped his hat as he backed away, raking the sand around us.

Oh God, we'd fallen asleep outside, under the stars.

I'd wanted to stay awake all night long, but the damn sleep fairy knocked me out. However, at some point I'd been covered up with a towel.

"Jon," I shook him awake, his eyes all puffy with sleep. "Hey."

He shot straight up, glancing at the time on his phone. "Oh my God, it's morning." He shuffled off the bed and grabbed our bag, stuffing the towel into it and unhooking the garbage bag. "I'm going to miss my shuttle."

Would that be so bad? I just sat there, frozen to the mattress. Whether I liked it or not, that moment had arrived. He was leaving. "Yeah, you'd better go." My body had turned to lead, and I could no longer move. Breathing suddenly became difficult.

In the midst of the rush, he stopped and dropped to his knees in the sand and rested his head on my thighs. "I'm so sorry. I don't want to go …"

My voice cracked. I'd been dreading this very moment for the past few days. "I know." A lump formed in the back of my throat. I ran my fingers through his hair and down over his back. There was so much pain between his shoulder blades, it reverberated into my hands. "You need to get going."

Slowly, he pushed himself up and his face was

filled with more sorrow and sadness than I could bear to look at. Instead of meeting his eyes, I stared into the sand.

"Meet me in the lobby." His voice was barely audible. "I need to pack, but I'll be there in fifteen minutes." A pleading look filled the pools of his ocean blues.

Feet in a hurry dug into the sand to get traction and off he went. My heart cracked in half seeing him dart away. It was over. My six days of paradise were crashing all around me like violent waves upon the shoreline.

"Tess," he called out and came running back to me. "Tess, I love you." He pulled me to my feet and kissed me until he couldn't anymore. "Ten minutes. Please."

"You need to go." I shooed him away and listened as he took off. Standing with what little strength I had, I picked up my bag and garbage and lumbered up to the resort. Although there was morning sun greeting everything with a smile, dark grey clouds would've been more appropriate. Each dragging step took me closer to our final goodbye. And I wasn't excited about that.

Chapter Twenty One

On the painful way up to the main floor of the resort, I remembered the keychain I'd bought for Jon, and suddenly my feet couldn't move fast enough. Rather than take the elevator from the pool level to the lobby, I pushed by some tourists and ran up the escalator, scaling the stairs two at a time while yelling out my apologies. The doors of the lobby elevator going up were just starting to close.

"Hold the doors, please." I ran as fast as my jelly legs could go and squeezed in just in time.

The elevator held a couple, a lovey-dovey couple who could've been on their honeymoon for all their sweet glances and the way their bodies were tightly pressed together. I had that and was about to lose it. I pushed button twenty-six repeatedly, hoping it would make it move faster. My foot tapped as the slowest-moving lift in history rose.

It chimed—finally!—and I raced out to my room,

having to insert the card into the lock three times before it unlocked and let me in. The room was still made up from yesterday. I dug through my cosmetic bag and searched in the vanity, trying to remember where I'd tucked that keychain away. Obviously, I'd put it someplace for safe keeping, and in my mad rush to find it, I'd forgotten.

"Damn it," I yelled.

I opened the drawer where I'd put my undergarments and swimsuits, and there, wrapped in the plastic bag, was the lazybones keychain and the note I'd written him one night when I couldn't sleep. Both items in hand, I raced back to the elevator. I had very little time left. Pacing over to the window, I checked outside. At the entrance was a long touring bus—the airport shuttle for guests.

"NO!" I banged on the window. The elevator chimed behind me and in record speed, I ran to it and jumped in, hammering the ground floor button.

"Please don't stop. Please don't stop." I made it down to floor eight before it halted. Which it did again at six. And at five. And at three. On the main floor, the doors opened, and uncharacteristically, although apologetically, I shoved my way through.

There were people mingling about in the lobby, but I didn't see him. Damn, how much time had I wasted?

"Jon!" I yelled out, running through the lobby and outside. "Jon!" I spotted him by the bus, loading his luggage into the belly of it. "JON!" I screamed at the top of my lungs.

He dropped his bag and turned around.

I ran and leapt into his arms, kissing him hard on the lips. "I love you."

"I love you," he said in between breaths and set me back on the ground. Only I would've preferred to stay in his arms.

"You can't leave before I give you this. I got this for you." I gave him the bag and note.

"Can I open it now?"

"Read the note later, but yes, open the package."

He didn't waste time, and the keychain dangled off his finger, looped through his ring finger. "I love it, thank you." He gave me another kiss, this one longer and with more passion. "I want you to go home a love-starved woman who won't be able to look at another guy without seeing me." He used my own line against me. Bugger.

"Too late," I whispered as tears built up. "I'll never be able to see any man. He won't be you."

A man in a floral print shirt and black shorts cleared his throat. "Time to go."

Jon embraced me in another kiss, so filled with

longing and lust and love and hunger that I would've turned my head had someone else been on the receiving end of it. But I didn't care. I was about to lose a piece of my heart as it flew back to Maine.

"I've got to go." Jon stepped away, still holding my hand.

"I know."

"I love you." The distance between us was growing as Jon neared the bus door.

"I love you." Our fingers were barely touching.

He stepped onto the bus and blew me a kiss. "I'll call you."

It was a pipe dream, one that'll never happen. The logistics of the whole thing would never work. Rivers of tears streamed down my face, and I blew a weak kiss back at him. This was goodbye. The end. It was over. Whatever we had would be chalked up to a vacation fling, something that I hoped in years to come I'd look back on fondly. But right now, my heart ached. For it all. For what could've been had there not been two countries separating us.

Jon disappeared behind the heavily tinted windows, and the doors closed up. With an awful shift, the bus dropped into gear and rounded the entrance, proceeding to drive away. Like the idiot I was, I stood there and waved, but I couldn't move off the sidewalk. The bus drove down the street and around a corner, completely taking him away.

A warm arm draped around me. "Come on. Let's get you inside."

"There goes the best thing to ever happen to me." I buried my head into Camille's neck and sobbed. Why had I let myself fall when I knew the end result would be painful?

We walked back into the lobby, and I allowed my best friend to guide me, unable to bear anymore pitying glances from the waiting guests.

"There you—" A deep voice started speaking. "Everything okay?"

"Can you give me an hour?" Camille asked.

I didn't know who that was, probably another fling, but I was grateful to Camille for not introducing me and allowing me to wallow for a bit.

We grabbed a table in the airy part of the buffet but I didn't eat. There were no food cravings, no desire to even munch on fruit. I just sat and sipped on a hot mug of coffee.

"A long-distance relationship can work."

"Right." My vision blurred while I gazed out to the ocean. "We're too far apart to make it work. Flights are stupid expensive, and we wouldn't be able to meet up very often. There has to be some end point to get us through, like me moving there or something, which would never happen, because he lives in another country. If he lived in Toronto, it would be much easier. But he's an American."

"I know." Her voice was soft.

"I can't make it work without that end point, and sadly," I smeared tears across my cheeks, "there isn't one for us."

"But there has to be. You guys have the real deal."

"It's not enough." I'd need to win the lottery to buy all the documents I'd need to work in the states and then move there, which I didn't know if I could do. My family and friends were here. Certainly, he could move to me, but the reverse was also true, his friends and family were there.

"Aren't you going to keep in contact?"

My heart further splintered, the crack growing deeper with each breath. "We'll try. But after a few months, it'll fade away, I'm sure. We can't do anything physical and FaceTime will only take us so far. It's not the same. We're pretty much over." A fresh batch of tears fell, and I pushed my coffee away.

Camille wrapped her hand around mine. "I'm sorry to hear that."

I was sorry to feel that, stupid girl I was. I knew I wouldn't be able to distance my heart from the reality. Damn it. I should've just stopped hanging out with him and not gotten so involved. What had I been thinking? That was the problem. I wasn't. I was led by my heart and feelings, and now I was paying for it. "You'd better eat up. When's your pickup coming?"

She checked her phone. "A couple of hours." With a flick of her head, she downed her morning cocktail.

I raised an eyebrow.

"What? You think I'm going to pay the overpriced cost of alcohol on a plane? No way. This is my last chance to get it for free." She rose. "And I need to make sure I'm filled up. Once I cross security, I'm at the mercy of junk food and high-priced water."

Camille loaded up her plate for a second time, and scarfed her food down, chasing it with another drink. Where she put her food, I'll never know. Her metabolism was off the charts.

As she finished up, I thought back over the week and all the fun I'd had. With Jon. I wrapped my arms around my chest as if it would keep my heart from jumping out and throwing itself to the floor in a final goodbye.

"Do you wanna walk me upstairs or would you rather just sit here alone in silence?"

"No, I'll see you off." I forced a small smile to my lips.

"Good, there's someone I want you to meet." She

linked her arm through mine as she stumbled through the restaurant. Guess her alcohol was kicking in.

We joined the other homeward bound tourists all hanging out in the lobby, murmurs and conversations in the air. The first bus for her pickup arrived, and the passengers all raced to line up.

Camille pointed at them. "What's the hurry? Why are they all rushing to be the first on the bus? It's not like they'll get to the airport any quicker. Besides, there are two buses."

Two lines formed, one to place their luggage, the other to board the bus. "Yeah, maybe they're just happy to go home."

"Yeah, maybe." She scanned around the lobby. "I'm not, so I'll be last. Besides, I'm waiting for someone."

"Camille," I said with a heavy heart. "I'm sorry I wasn't a better friend to you here."

"What are you talking about? I had a fabulous time." She gave my arm a rub.

"I ignored you for a guy. How lame am I?" I stared at her fancy espadrilles and sparkly toes while I leaned against her. "I'm a terrible friend."

"Hey. You stop that." She shook her shoulder out from under me. "You are an amazing friend, and if it wasn't for you even suggesting this trip, I wouldn't have been here to watch you fall in love."

My shoulders rolled in, and I crossed my arms over my chest. It didn't stop the pounding of my heart against my ribs.

"Besides, it wasn't all that bad. You weren't the only one who found somebody." Her voice piqued my interest.

"What?" I blinked at her a few times. Now, I really felt bad. I'd been so wrapped up in my own selfish world, I hadn't even noticed.

"Relax. I haven't fallen in love with this guy, but he's definitely—"

A tall guy who rated somewhat high on the hunky meter, strode over to us. "There you are." His voice was deep. "You about ready to fly home, Cammie?"

Camille winked at me and tucked a strand of hair behind her ear. "Don't look so surprised."

"But when?"

"Yesterday, and not to make you feel bad or anything, but what luck—he lives across town." She leaned closer and lowered her voice. "Last night we spent the evening hanging out in a cabana on this tiny section of private beach." Her gaze darted to the guy standing in front of us. "Right beside this other couple who thought they were being quiet as they had sex."

Heat bloomed in me and spread over my body, but I tightened my grip on my chest, hoping Camille wouldn't take note. Suddenly, it dawned on me that other couple Jon and I saw had been Camille and this guy. I gave him a once-over.

Not the typical guy Camille flirted over. He looked like a regular man, dressed nicely but not too sharp. Definitely didn't have that player vibe to him like the others she'd had fun with this week. His face was slightly familiar, but maybe only because I remembered seeing it quickly as he yanked the curtain across. If he recognised me, he stayed mum about it.

"Well, we've got to go." Camille grabbed her luggage. "I'll see you in three days."

I nodded.

"You'll be okay?"

"No. But I'm okay with that. I'll do some shopping and reading, and maybe I'll even have a drink for you." I gave her a tight hug and a kiss on the cheek.

She hugged me back with enthusiasm. "You'd better."

"Thank you. For everything."

"Love you." She swung her hips as she headed over to the one who waited for her.

I waved to her back and watched as her mystery

man loaded her luggage into the bus and helped her on. Maybe this guy would treat her better. I could only hope. Everyone deserved to find their happiness, and usually it happened when you least expected it.

Chapter Twenty-Two

"All finished," I said to no one. I'd just assembled a photobook complete with a diary of memories about my trip. Clicking send, I shipped it off to the printer. Someday I'd look back on it with nostalgia, for now, it was a simple reminder of what I had … and lost.

One by one, I closed the open tabs, leaving the background picture on my laptop to stare at me—the innocent picture of Jon and I on the beach of Troncones during our ATV ride. So new in knowing each other, and yet, so happy. I closed my eyes and remembered Jon's laughter, the sweet way he'd touched me after we'd collided into each other and fell into the ocean, and the way my heart just knew he was my destiny.

Not one to believe in karma or all that, I couldn't stop thinking about all the things that brought us together. Had I not booked that trip, had I tossed the note under the right door, would we still have met? The short answer was no. It was so highly unlikely that we would've crossed paths on the beach or on the boardwalk or at the theatre. We would've been two strangers who passed like ships in the night.

But the note *had* gone under his door, and he took the first step of coming down and being all sweet and charming. Life and love took off from there.

I closed my laptop. It wasn't going to happen. Jon lived in Maine, in the USA. I lived in Edmonton, in Canada. Two completely different places. I can't work in the US without being a citizen or having a work visa, but there wasn't a shortage of dental hygienists in America so getting a visa was out of the question. They won't give me a job if they have their own people. As frugal as I was, my savings wouldn't last me very long there and the reverse was true for Jon. Painful sighs rolled out of me. The whole situation was hopeless.

My phone chimed in with a text from Jon.

Hey, beautiful.

I typed back. *Hi*, and sent a wave GIF.

Can I call you? I need to see you and hear your voice.

Maybe it was for the best, and I could let him down and officially end what was the greatest week of my life. I begrudgingly typed back a yes and opened up my laptop.

Thirty seconds later, Jon's real time face replaced the photographic one.

"Hey," he said, a smile stretching across his face with his words.

"Hey." I readjusted the screen, wishing it was him I had my fingers around.

"I miss you."

"Same." The corner of my mouth twisted up in a weird smirk.

"You okay? You look …"

A soft snort fell out of me. "It's sadness, Jon. It's not knowing when I'll ever be able to see you again."

"You're seeing me now."

His attempt at humour was weak. My shoulders rolled forward, and I leaned closer to the screen. "Not the same thing."

"I know."

"Before you go any further, I need to get something off my chest."

His brows pinched together, and he held his breath.

"I think we need to end this. I'm not the type of person who can hold out and wait for something." I shook my head. "That came out wrong." Those ocean-blue eyes of his stared at me. "What I mean is, this relationship, us, I can't see how to make it work. You're never going to come to Canada and live, and I can't go there and live. We have no end goal that will work. All we can do is visit each other, like what, twice a year? I'm sorry, but that's not enough for me. I need to see you more than that. I need to feel you more than that. And I think it's best to end this before I completely fall apart."

"Really? Wow."

My focus left him and flittered over to the TV I had lurking on in the background. A rerun of the *Wonder Years* played.

"I'm sorry, Jon."

"Not as sorry as I am." He ran his fingers through his hair. "The only thing keeping us apart is the distance thing, right?"

I nodded. To me, that was it. If he lived in my country, I could find a way to make it work. Relocating would be tough, but doable. Another country though? Nearly impossible.

"I get that, really I do. But I don't want things over for us."

"I don't either." I ran my finger over his jaw. He couldn't see what I was doing, and it felt just as foreign. "I'm so torn. I want you, but I can't have you."

He sighed. "Yeah. I've been looking into that situation since I got home, trying to figure something out."

"It sucks." Tears blurred my vision.

"Oh, don't cry."

"I can't help myself." Every night since we'd separated I've cried myself to sleep and held my pillow tight against my chest, pretending it was Jon.

"Okay. Before you completely end it, can we make plans to get together? That would be a goal, right? Something to keep us moving forward while we work this out. Because, we need to make this work." He looked away briefly. "I can't tell you how lonely I've been since coming home. I'm missing something in my life, and you have it."

"I do?"

"Yeah. You have my heart, Tess."

Tears streamed down my cheeks. "Oh, Jon."

"Please tell me we can do this?" There was such sincerity on his face, it would've been hard for a strong person to say no to him. I wasn't strong at all and caved. "Let's make plans to meet at the end of June, okay? We can meet and discuss the future, what could work, what hasn't been working. Can you give us three months?"

Three long months. Ninety plus days. I wasn't sure if I could manage that long, but I wasn't truly ready to let him go. I nodded and barely breathed. "Okay."

"Okay?" His lips curved upwards as they stretched from ear to ear.

"Yeah, let's do it." I could make a long-distance relationship work for that time. It gave me an end point, for now.

The future beyond that was unsteady at best, but at least, for now, there was hope for Jon and me.

Chapter Twenty-Three

Camille tapped her foot against the long desk, where our receptionist typed furiously into the computer. "Tess, we're going to be late." It's a good thing the main doors had been locked.

"I know, I know," I said, bustling out of my hygienist's cubicle and poking my head around the corner. "I'm just finishing up." I ran a sanitising wipe over the last section of chair and mirror and lights. I was nothing if not meticulous in my cleaning.

The wipe flew across the air and landed in the garbage. Ten points for me.

"I just need to change."

"Hurry up. The lecture starts in forty minutes, and I still need to drive across town."

It wasn't that big a deal if we were late, was it? We were going to see a lecture on Greek Mythology and the Northern Constellations. Ever since getting home, I've kept an eye on the skies and even headed out to the local planetarium for a few shows, and checked out the local observatory. Of course, those astronomers all lacked Jon's charm and enthusiasm for the stars, but it was still neat to learn.

With my scrubs tucked into my bag, I stepped out of the change room wearing shorts and a V-neck T-shirt. "Better?" I looked to Camille for approval.

"It'll do." She shook her head. Camille was dressed like she was going to a dinner party in a nice dress and heels. She even had her hair done in a polished ponytail, something other than her standard issue messy bun. Her serious boyfriend had tamed her wildest ways, which after an unfortunate incident at school, had become toxic with all her drinking. "Come on." She looped her slender arm through mine.

I dropped my bag into the trunk of Camille's car and slipped into the passenger seat. My purse rested on my lap, but it started vibrating.

"Must be seven o'clock," Camille said with amusement in her voice.

Since our little agreement to get away together at the end of June, things between us strengthened. Every night at seven, my screen lit up with Jon's photo—the highlight of my day. I pushed the answer button.

"Hey, handsome."

His charming face smiled, and the dimple in his cheek deepened. "Hey, gorgeous. How was your day?"

"Same old business. Making everyone's smiles a little brighter and a whole lot cleaner."

Bells and dinging sounded around us as Camille started her car.

A deep V formed between his brows. "Are you at work?"

"Nah, Camille and I are heading to an astronomy lecture. Say hi." I turned the phone in Camille's direction.

"Oh. Hey, Camille."

"Hi, Jon." She put the car in reverse and backed out of the dental office's parking.

I twisted the phone back to face me.

"Is there a live show afterwards?"

"Not tonight." Sometimes, the lecturer would escort us out to the observatory for an up close and personal look on what we'd just learned on the giant dome. One night, we saw Jupiter through a telescope, and it was one of the coolest things I've seen. We saw the four moons in alignment and the red spot. "It's raining."

"Bummer. Makes it hard to see anything."

"That it does." I put my hand on the dash as Camille stomped on the brakes. "Geezus."

She bit her lip. "Sorry. Thought I'd make the light."

"Take it easy, Camille, that's my girl you're driving around."

"Yeah, yeah. I'll make sure she's still in one piece when you get here next week."

I nearly squealed with delight. "Six more days."

Our meetup wasn't going to be someplace exotic or fun. For the sake of expenses, we worked out a solution, a temporary one, that he'd come and spend a couple of weeks with me—he'd be able to work remotely—and at that point, we'd discuss me travelling to Maine either for the US Thanksgiving or Christmas. Total baby steps, but workable ones. It gave me something to focus on, and I liked that.

The sweet laughter from my best friend filled the interior of the car. "She's counting down the hours until your plane arrives."

"Am not." It was the total truth, I had a timer going on my phone. Last time I checked, there were still 150 hours until he touched down. I winked at Jon though. He knew better. He was just as excited and was also in countdown mode. The end of June felt like it would never arrive.

"It won't be long. I'm so looking forward to it," Jon beamed.

"Me too."

Camille grunted. "Get a room. Sheesh."

"Hey, did I tell you, someone is interested in my sightless technology?" Jon had been hard at work developing new software for the blind. "And they want to field test it."

"Wow, seriously? That's amazing. When does that start?"

"Don't have an official date yet, but probably in the fall. They're going to use some computer engineering students at the university to try it out."

A smile broke out across my face. "That's really great."

"Now if only modern medicine could find a way to slow the narrowing, I'd be all set." It was said matter-of-factly, but there was an underlining sadness in it. No one wanted to lose their vision, not when there was so much beauty to see in the world.

"Maybe someday."

"It'll be too late."

"Maybe when you're up here, we can check out some specialists. They might be on the edge of something." Someone somewhere had to have developed something to slow his tunnel vision, and needed a willing participant to test it on. There had to be.

He shrugged, but a sly smile tickled the edge of his lips and crinkled his eyes. "I'd rather check out other things."

"I'm still here, Jon," Camille said.

"I said that for your benefit." He laughed.

I missed that laugh, and I missed holding him and touching him and breathing him in. He must've known what I was thinking. "Soon, Tess. Soon. I promise."

"I know." A lump started to form in the back of my throat. This long-distance relationship was so hard.

"Got to go. Talk to you tomorrow." He blew me a kiss. "Love you."

"Love you too." I blew a kiss back.

He said goodbye to Camille before he hung up. She gave my thigh a squeeze. "Six more days. You've got this. Why don't we go shopping tomorrow and find something sexy for your first night together? There's this great place downtown that sells naughty but nice lingerie."

"That sounds good." I stared out the window, and made mental notes about what I needed to get done before his arrival. Yes, shopping for new lingerie topped the list, but I wanted to show him off to the world and show him my beautiful city. Sure, I didn't live in the tropics, but it had some amazing architecture and bridges, and a lush river valley. We could have a picnic by the river ...

"We're here."

The planetarium was a round theatre with reclining chairs to give you a better view of the dome above.

Camille and I took our seats in the middle of the theatre where the seats reclined the most, rendering us almost flat. The stars all danced above us, taking me back to a warm, Mexico night. A few minutes after we settled in, the lights dimmed and a smattering of twinkling stars filled up the screen over our heads.

A soothing voice spoke about tonight's topic on Greek Mythology and, using a laser pointer, marked out the constellations and how they came to be.

I tapped Camille on the arm when he mentioned Cassiopeia.

The male voice talked about the Queen's endless vanity in her thinking how she was beyond beautiful, and that her daughter was evermore stunning. So much so, without even trying, she angered the Gods.

"And in needing to appease Poseidon, the God of the Sea, Cassiopeia needed to sacrifice her daughter, Andromeda, to the sea monster, Cetus." The red laser outlined the constellation Cetus, making it a little clearer to me where that was in relation to the galaxy I was most familiar with.

I gave Camille's arm another tap and whispered, "This is the best story."

"That's where our hero steps in. The mighty Perseus …" The laser outlined the eleven brightest stars. "Who was on his way back from killing Medusa."

The crowd gasped. The interpreter was good, but he was no Jon.

Lines connected the dots, adding a cartoonish outline to the constellations - the Queen, the Princess, the sea monster and the warrior all taking shape. "He stumbled upon the beautiful Andromeda, who's chained to a rock just as Cetus is about to claim her. But he defeats the sea monster and rescues the princess."

I beamed over at Camille. "Pretty amazing, eh?"

She shrugged, and even in the dark I knew she rolled her eyes. She only joined me on these lectures because I begged and pleaded. "I guess. Would've been better if Andromeda had swiped Perseus's sword and stabbed the sea monster herself."

Someone behind us clapped and agreed.

"It's just a story." Leave it to Camille to put a more modern spin on the tale, rather than enjoy it for what it was, a fictional story.

The theatre operator stopped talking, and I shrunk

into my seat. It was like being busted in high school for talking out of turn.

"It was a love written in the stars, and one no one could've predicted. There was Perseus, strolling along, minding his own business. Perhaps Andromeda was trying to free herself from the chains that tied her down. Always trying to be in control, she never wanted to admit that she was scared. And who knows, maybe Perseus hid to the side and watched her for a while, captivated by her beauty, but in seeing her strength, knew without a doubt he needed to—not rescue her per se—but help her."

I curled into my seat a little more. Surely, he'd heard our whisperings.

"Fun fact …"

My heart did a double beat and I clamoured out to the edge of my seat, looking around the dark theatre while holding my breath. The interpreter was in the booth across the dome from me, and it was so hard to see his face.

"Did you know that prior to Andromeda being chained to the rock, she was already promised to another man?"

That voice was so familiar. But how? Where? It wasn't possible. He was still in Maine. I'd talked to him an hour ago. He was in his apartment.

"But she did not marry that guy. Eventually, in

time though, Andromeda and Perseus got married and produced seven sons and two daughters."

A spotlight flickered to the opposite side of the theatre, and my heart nearly blew up. Standing in a suit, holding a microphone and walking toward me was my own real-life Perseus. And he looked utterly amazing.

"Ladies and Gentlemen, I'd like you to meet my Andromeda." He strutted over to me wearing a grin that was larger than life and offered his hand.

It was real, and soft, and warm. I linked my fingers through his and rose, tremors of trepidation making my knees a little weak. With wobbly steps, he guided me up onto the small platform in the center of the theatre. Glancing at Camille, she shrugged nonchalantly, and that telling smirk on her face meant she knew.

"True love is real. And it does happen when you least expect it. I hope that your love for each other lasts as long as the stars, and that the light between you never diminishes. Thank you for attending the show. Refreshments are being served in the star room through which you entered." Using the laser pointer, he circled the entrance and clicked off the microphone.

I couldn't focus on anything else. He was so much more charming in the flesh than over the quality of an iPhone, with a smile so deep, his dimple threatened to become a black hole. "Hey." That was the best I could say.

"I couldn't wait six more days."

"Clearly." I wanted to jump into his arms and passionately kiss him, but there were still people mingling about. "How did …"

His gaze momentarily flickered over to Camille but came back to me. "It's been in the works for a while. Turns out, after doing some digging, I found out my mom was born in Toronto but moved to the US when she was six months old. It's a little complicated, but I applied for a permanent residency card, and I get to stay."

"Oh, wow." It was really happening. A dream come true to have an end goal, and know that our relationship was moving onto bigger and better things. My heart pounded with excitement as my brain tried to process everything Jon was telling me.

"After learning that, I submitted my proposal for the seeing-impaired technology and your university picked it up. We've been in discussions, and they're going to move me to a space on campus. They were a huge help with my immigration application. I even already have a job, here, giving talks on the stars as a guest speaker."

"What?" I would've seen his name on the program.

"I asked them to keep it hush until tonight." He beamed and wrapped his arms around my waist, pulling me closer. "Got my immigration papers all handled, my accommodations taken care of, and a job to boot."

"When?" I pinched myself, hoping I wasn't dreaming. "When did you start working here?"

"Last night. I flew in yesterday."

"You knew?" Wide-eyed, I peered at Camille, who was still seated in her chair, a smug expression on her face. Oh yeah, she knew. Probably had a hand in planning it all too.

"Guilty."

"My dorm room isn't ready yet, but I'm staying at a hotel near here. But the absolute best part of this whole thing is that I get to see you every single day in the flesh."

I clasped my hands behind his head and pulled him down for a kiss. "That is the best news I've ever heard. However ..."

He pulled back and stared into my eyes.

"Do you have to live on campus? There's half of my bed that's available."

He kissed me back and tightened his grip around my waist. "Are you sure?"

"Nothing would please me more, my Perseus."

"Andromeda." The word was like a song on his lips, and it was music to my soul.

Epilogue

We sat in the doctor's office, holding hands tightly, while Dr. Bingham scrolled through the test results.

"Are you positive?" Jon asked again, relief wanting to be on the tip of his tongue.

"I've checked out your history, consulted with your other doctor in Maine and reviewed your files. Based on the extensive tests you've done with me, yeah, I'm happy to tell you that there's been no change to your vision, and if I dare say it, a very marginal improvement."

I squeezed Jon's hand. This was the good news he'd been hoping for. He'd had three appointments over the last seven months, each checking something different.

"For three years, my vision tunnelled. And it's really stopped?"

"I know it sounds miraculous, but sometimes these things happen."

"So, I won't be blind in a few years?" There was shock mixed with total euphoria in his voice. Coming to see the world-renowned Dr. Bingham had been a stroke of luck, he'd been one of the doctors on the board who was interested in Jon's technology and offered to take him on as a new patient.

Dr. Bingham tapped on his keyboard for a few clicks, and then leaned against the cabinetry. "Officially, I can't say that it won't eventually happen, but off the record, you have a great possibility of your vision staying like it is for the rest of your life."

"Wow, doc, I'm in shock." He rose and enthusiastically shook his doctor's hand. "For real? This isn't a prank?"

"No prank, I promise." The doctor clapped him on the shoulder. "Your night vision might suffer, but so far all signs appear stable. And that's the best prognosis."

"No kidding." Jon's face was lit up, and the blue of his eyes sparkled under the florescent lighting. His hand twitched with energy. "Thank you."

"My pleasure." He logged out of the screen and exited the room.

Feeling Jon's happiness, I wanted to run all the way home and put that spirit to good use. "What shall we do now?" I wiggled my eyebrows at him. There was a dirty list a mile long that I'd like to cross off one by one, but real life and adulting had to happen first.

"Well," he held open the car door for me, "I have to drop by my client's house first and pick up a few files. Shouldn't take too long. After that, the rest of my Saturday is free."

"Great, 'cause I have big plans for you later."

"Oh, really?"

"Yep." I fastened my seatbelt. "I went shopping with Camille." I pulled my bra strap out of my shirt to show him. It was black with white speckles.

He gave it a quick peek and put the car in gear.

"When you see the whole thing, you'll be able to hold a galaxy in the palm of your hand."

That got his attention. "Now I look forward to seeing the rest."

"I figured you'd like it."

We drove through the city and out onto the highway.

"Where exactly is this client of yours?" We were headed west. If he kept going that way for four hours, we'd hit Jasper; an idyllic mountain town where we'd gone downhill skiing for the first time ever. The fact that I hadn't broken a bone was encouragement for a repeat trip.

"Sorry, Charlie's shop is out in Spruce Grove. I

wanted to get a feel for his store so I can implement that onto his website."

"Gotcha."

We pulled up to a little strip mall and parked in front of a store called Butterflies and Bulldogs, all decorated in bright colours.

"Is this a children's store?"

"Yeah. He wants to be able to sell the clothing and accessories online, but he's struggling with the revolving inventory and all that." He led the way to the door. "Oh, and he's a little eccentric, so if he asks you something out of the ordinary, just go with the flow."

"How about I wait in the car?"

Jon mock pouted. "Really? He's like a cross between Dr. Janosh from *Ghostbusters* and Doc Brown from *Back to the Future*."

Well, that I had to see.

As I stepped through the door, harps played in the overhead speaker, and a small wooden bridge over a painted stream led us into the main part of the store. But this was no ordinary store. Full length murals of castles and rolling hills surrounded us. Under a tent, constructed to look like a flea market, were racks of clothes. Little mushroom stools were everywhere, and in the centre was a little castle turret, and a sign that read, Change Room.

"Oh my God, kids must love it here." I wondered if Camille had ever been in here, her kindergarten students would lose their minds in the wonder of it all.

"Oy, there." A short man about five feet tall, if that, with Einstein-like hair, dressed in wizard robes, came charging in our direction, and turned us around, pushing us back toward the door. "All adults must put on one accessory if they are to be in the store. It's the rules." He pointed at a large wardrobe we'd missed. "It's for the children, see." There was a heavy Dutch accent.

Jon raised an eyebrow in my direction and shook his head while opening the cupboard doors. He grabbed a purple cone-shaped hat with colourful streamers and passed it to me.

I laughed and fastened it to my head, adjusting the Velcro-ended elastic. Surely, I was going to knock something off a top rack as the hat was at least two feet high.

"Oh, and this." He wrapped a cape around me. It was a pink satin number with sparkly stars on it. "Perfect."

"What about you?" There wasn't much in there that would suit a man. Must be a lot of moms or aunts that shop here with their kids.

He moved some items around and found a foam sword and shield, holding them up for my approval.

"At least it's not pink." I hated that colour, even though I was now decked in it from shoulder to feet.

"Oh, here we go." Jon pulled out a plastic knight hat, with a yellow feather sticking out the top and crammed it onto his head. "That's better."

"Careful, you'll break it. And then what will the other dads wear?"

Jon looked utterly ridiculous, and yet kind of cute. It was endearing, and Jon was right, the owner was a little off his rocker to be so demanding of his patrons.

We paraded back into the shop and over to the desk. The sides were painted to look like a bridge with trolls lurking around it.

"You must be Charlie?" Jon asked.

"No, it's King Charles." He tapped around his desk and pulled out a golden crown and placed it upon his greying poof of hair. "Welcome to my fairy tale."

"It's great to meet you in person. Jonathan Baker." He set the sword onto the counter and stuck out his hand.

"Ah, yes, my web developer. How do you do?" He gave a slight handshake. "You see what I mean when I say I need something better than the standard website? Kids come here to play and have fun getting new clothes."

If only this kind of place had existed when I was younger.

I inched away from the business talk and over to the 'market.' Cute little princess dresses with poufy skirts hung on the rack. I flipped a tag over on one of the less expensive-looking tulle and satin creations and read the cost. How does anyone afford such an expense for their kids? It was of play quality, and yet, he wanted $150 for the dress. Yikes. Would also explain why the store was so quiet.

King Charles and Jon were engrossed in deep conversation, so I wandered around the store, marvelling at the artistry that went into all the paintings. The place was huge, much bigger than my dental office, that's for sure. With a few additions of indoor playground furniture, he could have quite the place here. Fun for the kids and shopping for the parents, if he lowered his prices.

A trumpet blared through the speaker, and I covered my ears. That needed a much lower volume too. Perhaps it would be better if I sat in the car and waited. I could figure out what to plan for supper. After all, we had a reason to celebrate. I strolled past the painted castle, dangling my fingers across the plastic gates and turned at the change room turret.

My jaw hit the floor. Oh my God, what was he doing? And why here of all places? We looked ridiculous. On bended knee, Jon held up a ring.

"Tess, in all the lands I've searched for a princess who would accept me for who I am and who I'd become, and I've never met another who is as noble and loving and tender as you. Would you do me the honour of being my better half for as long as we both shall live?"

Tears flooded down my cheeks and I stepped closer to him, nodding. "Yes. Yes. Yes." I cupped his whiskery face and my fingers touched the edges of his plastic knight helmet, kissing him on the lips as I parted mine and begged for more.

Jon pulled back and stared into my soul. "You have no idea how happy you make me." He pulled the ring free from the box and slipped it onto my finger. I was not shaking or trembling, but I knew why.

I dug into the pocket of my dress and pulled out the ring I'd purchased for him. "Oh, I think I do."

His eyes went large as he took in the ring. "What? Really?" The sweetest laugh caressed my ears.

"I was going to suggest a walk through the river valley, near our spot, but you beat me, damn it." His hand trembled as I pushed the rose-gold coloured ring on. "I love you so much, Jon. I couldn't imagine loving anyone more." For good measure, I kissed him again. "You are my knight in shining armour," I pointed to his sword and helmet, "I didn't think I needed in my life. But every moment with you has been a gift, and I'm so glad I threw caution to the wind and booked a last-minute trip to Mexico. I'm even happier that the note went under your door and you responded to it."

"I'm so glad too." There were tears in his eyes.

"And we'd better have our wedding there."

"At sunset."

I shook my head, the ribbons from my princess hat softly floating around me. "Nope, when Andromeda and Perseus are perfectly positioned in the sky."

A giant smile cracked his face in half. "A nighttime wedding would be perfect. It would be us."

"It would be made in the stars."

IT ALL BEGAN
with a mai tai

The freeze-your-lungs-solid temperature in the covered jetway was a stark contrast to the sweaty, re-circulated tropical interior of the plane, unloading its Mexican tourists none too eager to step foot back into their native winter land. A 45 °C swing in the span of a few hours was a less than ideal way to return home. Just lovely. Thankfully, I had the hindsight to pack a sweater in my carry-on bag, and I pulled it tighter across my chest.

I took a long look at my handsome and charming, albeit tired, traveling companion as we stepped off the jetway and wandered through the airport, over to the luggage pick up. Back on the resort, he'd been the guy who captured my attention the longest, and lucky for me, he lived across town.

"Anyone picking you up?" I asked Will. He seemed like the guy who family was important to, and surely one of them would be there.

"My sister, Janet." He hoisted his carry-on bag over his shoulder and held my hand a little tighter. "You?"

I bit my lip. Normally, it would be my bestie, but she was still back in Mexico. My family and I don't get along very well, and a few years back I raised some hell and was since abandoned. Oh well. It didn't bother me.

"I'm going to cab it home." And I hoped no one showed, although another friend had offered. I wanted the romantic fantasy; the one I'd watched on the tv screen. The long lingering kiss goodbye, foot tipped up in the air, the don't want to you let go waves, the promise of getting together again…

"We could give you a ride."

"That's really sweet, but I'm on the west side and you're out in the Park district."

He gazed down upon me. "It's no big deal."

He was so sweet, willing to drive twenty-five minutes to my house and then an additional thirty to his. But it was too much. "I'll think about it."

"Excellent." He lit up like a Christmas tree. "You'll love my sister. She's super sweet, and looks just like me, except she's feminine." I couldn't imagine the tall, dark haired Will with any feminine features. Did his sister have a strong jaw line with the more-than-a-hint of five o'clock shadow? I truly hoped not.

We got into the customs line and having cleared it, went over and grabbed our luggage. Will travelled light; one small suitcase. He pulled my industrial-sized pink bag—that I had to pay additional for—off the conveyor belt and smiled as he rolled it to me. That smile bagged me the first time I saw it spread across his face. Every time it happened, I was like putty in his hand.

"Just the one, right?"

I originally packed two suitcases, but my bestie talked me down to one big one. My pleas for another rolled off deaf ears. The horror of horrors if I was caught in the same dress twice in one week, vacation or not. Same with swim wear, although if I was honest, the bikinis didn't take up much room. But she was right. Damn her. Nodding, I tugged on the handle of my suitcase and walked toward the main entrance where family and friends greeted you as if you were a famous celebrity. I thrust my weary shoulders back and tipped my chin up.

"We're still on for dinner Monday night?" he asked, stopping to let me pass first through the double doors.

"Absolutely." Our plans had been of a romantic nature; dinner at a quiet restaurant after a full day back to work with an expensive bottle of wine, maybe a little night cap afterwards…

"Great. I'll need to see a friendly face after work. It's tough meeting new colleagues."

"Where do you work?"

That should've been a conversation we'd already had, but back in Mexico it was nice to just simply enjoy the presence of another human being without having to fill the conversation with mindless chatter. Instead we shared space, shared kisses and shared knowledge that we were comfortable with each other. For me, that never happens. But with Will something just clicked.

The double doors automatically opened before he answered and the area before us was filled with loved ones, ready to welcome home their travelling friends and family. I was envious of them since no one stood there waiting for me. However, I still sauntered past the crowds, trying to appear as if I didn't care. I brushed the wavy strands of hair off my shoulders and put a grin on my face that I knew was a smidgen of alluring mixed with a bit of spice.

"There's Janet," Will said, giving my hand a little tug and pulling me away from the crowd that in my dreams thought I was someone famous.

I scanned the crowds looking for a mini-Will, and that's when I spotted it on the other side of the railing. A large sign held above the crowd that read CAMILLE EVANS. Trey, my cheating boyfriend who'd been negligent on the romance as of late, stood smiling underneath it. Until he spotted me holding Will's hand.

"Oh damn."

Will pointed to the sign, his cheery disposition hitting the floor like a raindrop. "That's you?"

I nodded.

"And that's your brother, right?"

From the pitch in his tone, it was a question he hoped the answer was yes. I hated that I was going to disappoint him.

Three days.

That's all I seemed I was going to get with perfect Will. With a guy who was tender and fun, and didn't look at me like I was a piece of meat. Inhaling, and debating on lying, which was far beneath me, I answered with honesty. There was no hint of happiness in my voice, only disgust. "I can explain. That's my boyfriend."

Will released my hand faster than if he'd been shocked. "Seriously?"

I shrugged and a painful smile hung out on my lips. It was all I had left.

"Don't ever call me." He stormed a few feet away. "Ever." Turning around, he stopped and faced me, hurt crawling across his tight features. "I thought you were different."

I stuck my foot out and crossed my arms over my chest. No way was I going to look like the bad one here, even if I was. "You picked me up, remember?"

Will and I had met at the adults only pool when he walked by with a handful of drinks. I'd already had too much to drink and thought he was my waiter, so I flagged him down. He was wearing a white shirt like the other employees and had a thick mop of dark, wavy hair and a tan so golden, well, let's just say, he fit the part. It was an honest—drunken—mistake. Anyway, Will dropped off the drinks for his intended party friends and came back with the Mai Tai I'd ordered. Upon closer inspection, he wasn't staff. They weren't built like lifeguards and fireman.

Will stared and his mouth opened, however words failed to fall out. Instead, he took a step back, and spun on his heel.

"Wait, I am different." But it was useless, and I was above begging.

He walked over to his shorter sister, who bore a slight resemblance to him, and the two of them glared at me. More so her than him.

A pitiful I-can-only-blame-myself sigh rolled out of me. What was done, was done. I knew better than to fight a losing battle.

Flipping my gaze in Trey's direction, he wasn't looking thrilled either. The sign was on its side, and Trey was leaning on it.

"Hey," I groaned as I walked over. The suitcase came to a rest beside me and I sat upon it, the weariness of the day starting to take its toll. I should've been smarter to think that Trey would be affectionate after seeing me holding hands with another guy, but still. The fact that he didn't even lean in for a quick peck stung. I'd always kissed him after his indiscretions.

"Him? You were snogging him?"

Well... Will wasn't someone I snogged with. Not so much. He was more like an old soul trapped in a young man's body; a gentleman. Unlike the other resort guys I'd had the pleasure of meeting, Will was more of a hold your hand and kiss you at the end of the night kind of guy. Disappointingly, we hadn't even made it to third base so the snogging part was still a ways a way. Except now I'll never know how he was in bed, and he'll never learn how amazing I am. Yes, there were others at the resort, at the beginning. Two for sure, but to use Trey's favourite term, they meant nothing.

My head tipped to the side as I stretched out my aching neck muscles. "What's good for the goose is good for the gander." I met his glare head on.

"For real?"

"Oh right, because you didn't the entire week I was away?" I laughed. "I may be blonde, but I'm not a complete idiot."

He pulled back in surprise.

My voice peaked. "Trust me, stud, I know more than you think I do. I know about Maria and Angelica and Jordyn."

It was fun watching him pale a little, especially since there were people mingling around us, checking out the conversation. He hated being the center of attention, where I loved it.

"Oh yeah, I know." Thanks to my little spy friend at the Pine Tree, I knew all about the indiscretions, and for whatever weird and wild reason, they never bothered me. I just kept a list of dates and times, and always wore a condom. I was the consistent one, the fall back one, the one he always came back to. And I was okay with that. However, I played his game while I was gone, and I had to admit, there was something fun about a different guy each day. No expectations for more. Just truly a wham-bam-thank-you-m'am kind of fun. A revenge cheat. Or two.

Except, I hadn't planned on encountering a guy like Will. I didn't think I'd ever find a guy I could envision spending the rest of my life with. History said second best was all I was good enough for.

"What do we do now?" Trey just stood there, like a deer in the headlights. The sign was starting to curve under his lean.

Will and Janet had walked away without another glance back, and my heart ached with each passing breath. For a moment in time, even if it was only three days, Will had given me hope that I could be treated like a lady. That I was worthy of being treated so. He was the first guy in a long, long time who made the butterflies in my stomach soar and my heart beat a little faster.

In one fell swoop the fantasy was gone, and in its place was Trey. He was my fallback just as much as I was his, maybe even more so. A safety net that no matter what happened, he'd still be around. This incident was proof.

Exhausted from a day of travelling, a loud heaviness breathed out of me. "Take me home." I tugged on my luggage and headed toward the parking lot. "It's high time you and I discussed some things."

IT ALL BEGAN
with a wedding

Thursday – June 11th

I was minutes away from becoming the sole owner of a national chain of pharmacies. I was minutes away from becoming richer than I ever dreamed. I was minutes away from my life changing forever. The worst part was, I wanted nothing to do with it.

"Miss Richardson, are you hearing what I'm saying?" The oldest-looking of the three men pulled off his wire-rimmed glasses, and with his other hand rubbed the bridge of his nose.

"Yes, sir."

"Would you care to repeat it back to me? This is a very important matter and it's imperative that you fully understand." He glanced to the other two people; each one sitting on the other side of him – all three staring across the table at me.

Carefully, and with the intent of coming across as

much older than my twenty-seven years, I nodded. "If I'm to understand you correctly…" I glanced at the folders lined up neatly between us. "I am about to inherit my grandfather's shares of his pharmaceutical company Merryweather-Weston."

I didn't add that it was a company my grandfather Lloyd Merryweather started from the ground up in his late teens in the 1960's. When he married my grandmother Thelma Weston in 1965, he added her name to the business. Together, over the past fifty years, they grew their mom and pop corner store into a nationwide chain.

"That's correct." He reached for a file and opened it to a pinned page. "Go on."

I kept my sighs to myself. "As the, how did you put it, shareholder with the largest interest, I will hold 58% of the company's shares and stocks which are currently held in the family trust." My math was rusty and the numbers I'd written down at the start of the meeting were swimming around on the page. All I knew was that by having more than fifty percent, I was in charge, another thing I wasn't looking forward to. Running a business was so beyond my learning capabilities. Why hadn't Grandpa bothered to discuss this with me previously? Oh right. He wasn't supposed to have been killed.

An older gentleman, originally introduced as the

accountant, who sat next to the lawyer, scribbled across a legal pad. "The correct percentage is 58.3." He didn't lift his eyes to make contact with me.

That's what that number was. I circled it repeatedly to drive that home. Percentages with decimals were a big deal. As I looked around the boardroom, I was so out of my league, and every person in that room knew it. Growing up the way I did, I wasn't expected to follow in my single mother's footsteps and eventually run the business the way she had, not even when cancer took her away four years ago. She'd been on board though when I felt a calling into micro-biology and creating new drugs that would cure various illnesses. I wanted to be famous for finding a cure for cancer, not running a well-known business.

Instead of toiling away in the lab, I was sitting with a lawyer, an accountant and whoever the third guy was, forced to take ownership of the entire three thousand plus stores. Although the way they talked about the whole situation, it was already a done deal. They just needed my signature on a bunch of papers to make it official.

"Just so you're aware, Mr. Pratt, I know—"

"We are aware of your position, Miss Richardson. With Mr. Merryweather's accident, this has been thrust upon you. The board of directors are willing to assist you however they can until you get on your feet, and the CEO is on board to bring you up to speed. This meeting is just to sign over the documents that will make you the President."

I cleared my throat. "And if I decide that I don't want to be the president of the company?" I belonged in the lab, wearing latex gloves and eye goggles, not in a boardroom, running a company. However, with my family all gone, it appeared like I had little choice in the matter.

That blank look the lawyer had for the last hour hadn't faded with my admission. "You are free and clear to sell off your shares as you see fit, after first offering them to the board of directors." He flipped through a stack of papers and retrieved a stapled package and set it in front of me.

There was so much I needed to learn. Why did Grandpa have to drive that day? If he'd only taken a ride from his service... I shook my head, feeling a tendril of hair sneak out of the clip and fall across the nape of my neck. So much for maintaining a professional look.

"Miss Richardson," said the only man in the room who really hadn't talked much over the past hour. So many different terms had come and gone that I couldn't remember what his position was. "If I may." He pulled himself closer to the table and set down his pen. "This is a difficult time for you, and we're all aware how much information you are being bombarded with."

At least someone had the decency to understand.

"In simple terms, you are now the sole owner of your grandfather's company and you can be as involved as you wish. However, any changes you'd like to implement must pass through the board. The twelve members collectively hold the other 41.7% of the business. None of that will change, unless you wish to sell part or all of your shares. The only thing that has changed, at this point in time, is the name on the title. Merryweather-Weston will continue to operate in its excellent way with or without your input."

My head was swirling with words and numbers and visions of a stuffy board room similar to the one I was in and a future where I'd be swimming with the sharks. Oh, how I needed to escape, even if just for a moment to catch my breath. There were no windows up here, no view to take in. Just dark grey walls giving the whole room an institutional feel. I twitched in my seat and buried my head in my hands.

"I'm sorry, I just need time to process all of this. To be honest, I thought I was coming here to sign a few papers." I wanted to add and *go my merry* way but refrained and bit my lip instead.

The lawyer broke his staidness and cocked an eyebrow in my general direction.

The last guy pulled back another file with a tab that had my name on it and opened it. A stack of papers at least a half inch thick were neatly tucked inside. Were those all on me?

An unknown and unwelcome tightness squeezed around my chest.

A knock sounded on the door.

"Come in," the lawyer said.

A middle-aged man in a form-fitting suit walked in and dropped another file on the table. "Sorry to interrupt, but we found some information that changes the presidency of the company."

"Miss Richardson, this is Mr. Colby Pratt, one of the board members."

Mr. Pratt shook my hand with a giant Cheshire cat grin and turned his attention back to the lawyer. I'd never met the man previously, but his name was one tainted from overhearing Grandpa discuss business over the phone when he was at home. Mr. Pratt name did not come with the affection of a grandfather talking with a grandson, instead it was met with disdain. Grandpa wanted Mr. Pratt out of the business but he refused to sell.

"What did you find out?"

Mr. Pratt did not glance in my direction. "At the time of Ms. Nora Weston's passing, Mr. Merryweather updated his last will and testament and named Miss Richardson here as the sole inheritor."

Nora Weston was my mother, their former CEO and president who was as tough as nails.

"We have already established that."

"However, those shares are to be halved." Mr. Pratt puffed out his chest, straining the buttons on his already too-tight shirt. "As a lawyer, how did you not check out Miss Richardson's person?" He narrowed his eyes. "According to the Matrimonial Property Act, her shares would be equally split between her and husband, effectively diluting the ownership. With that division, including her shares owned previously, she would own 34.45% of the shares. As a shareholder with a personal share total of 35%, that would mean I'd become president." He pushed a stapled copy of papers in the lawyer's direction.

Matrimonial Act? Was that something that worked out between Grandpa and Grandma? No wait a minute, he was referring to *my* shares. But I wasn't married.

I still hadn't even found the guy I'd want to share anything personal with, let alone spend the rest of my life with him. Married? The idea was crazy enough to make me laugh. But I held back.

Wait a minute!

Images flitted through my mind at light-speed. A cute guy. A convention back in the fall. Way too much booze.

The lawyer lifted the new document and flipped through them. "But she hasn't announced an engagement, Mr. Pratt. I think you're jumping the gun just a little, and if she were to get married, she can, and should, get a prenuptial." He looked down his nose at me.

"She's already married."

Everyone knew that marriages in Vegas were a farce. There needed to be a license and all that. One can't simply go into any old chapel and get married without those things. Otherwise, it's like performing a part of a play; it wasn't real.

Mr. Michael's stupid grin got even bigger when he turned to me.

I balled my hands into tight little fists. Fight with the truth, Grandpa said, and you'll always win. "It wasn't legal." I inhaled and tried to calm myself down. "Where's the marriage license?"

Mr. Pratt flipped through his file and dropped a single piece of paper on the table between the lawyer and myself.

Clear as a bell on a beige wedding certificate from the Cupid's Arrow Chapel was my name and the name of one Theodore Breslin.

That drunken night at a Vegas medical conference flashed through my mind again. There was no way anyone would've married us, we were too drunk to know how to spell our names, as evident in the spelling of mine. On the certificate, my name was spelled I-S-A-B-E-L-L-A, but in truth, the 's' was a 'z'.

The buttons on my blouse pulled against their holds as I inhaled rapidly. I couldn't be married. It can't be possible. I haven't even seen that guy since then.

"Miss Richardson?" The lawyer's voice seemed far away as if caught in a fog.

My hand wiped the building sweat off my forehead, taking all my composure with it. "Yeah?" Grandpa would've smacked my backside for answering an elder like that.

"I guess that solves your dilemma."

"What's that?"

"You said you didn't want to be president, and now you don't have to worry about that. You'll remain on board as a minor shareholder, but not the president."

It sounded as if I should've been happy about the news of a marriage to a guy I didn't recall saying I do to, but the smug look on Mr. Pratt face wiped away the smidgen of joy I may have held for the briefest of heartbeats. Not only did he resemble a weasel, he acted like it too. A burst of adrenaline coursed through me. Yeah, maybe I didn't want to run the company, but I'll be damned if I was going to turn it over to him. Grandpa really disliked him.

I faced the lawyer. "If I get a divorce, how does that work?"

"By law, if there was no prenup, he'd still be entitled to half."

Right, that whole Matrimonial Act and all. That wouldn't solve issue number one. I needed to think. A drunken marriage. I was sure there were more of those than not. How many ended up not being legit? Probably low. I tapped my head. Wasn't there a celebrity who married in Vegas and got it annulled?

"What about an annulment? Then that would dissolve the marriage and all assets remained would be mine, correct?"

Mr. Pratt's face fell. Good.

The lawyer shuffled a few papers around and scribbled on his legal pad. "Provided you and..." He reached for the marriage certificate. "Mr. Breslin met certain criteria."

"Like? Is being drunk enough to not remember reason enough?"

"It stacks the deck in your odds." He finally made eye contact with me but after first glancing up at Mr. Pratt.

The prick had the audacity to laugh. "She'll never get in front of a judge in time."

"Why's that?"

"Because Miss Richardson..." He opened his file and flipped to a page tagged with a yellow tab, "if you'd read section 198.14, and I'll summarize this for you, it basically states that even though the estate is frozen, there is a 60 day grace period to find an interim president. With your assets now in half, I legally become the president, and there are only fifteen days left to contest." I could almost imagine Grandpa saying he'd smack that look off the smug bastard's face. The thought made me smile.

"Well, let's get that process started, so I can get before a judge. I'll need a minute with you, in private, please," I addressed the lawyer.

"Absolutely."

An hour later, I left the high rise building in the heart of our downtown a different person. Not only was I married, but I had a less than two weeks to find my husband, get an annulment before the judge Mr. Pratt had graciously set up for me, and retain major shares in the business I barely understood in order to keep Mr. Pratt greasy little hands off it. In a couple of hours, I'd aged ten years.

H.M. Shander Books

Duly Noted – book 1
That Summer – book 2
If You Say Yes – book 3
Serving Up Innocence
Serving Up Devotion
Serving Up Secrecy
Serving Up Hope
It All Began with a Note
It All Began with a Mai-Tai
It All Began with a Wedding
Noel
Whistler's Night
Dreamers in Cheshire Bay
Return to Cheshire Bay
Adrift in Cheshire Bay
Awake in Cheshire Bay
Christmas in Cheshire Bay
Journey to Cheshire Bay
Charmed in Cheshire Bay
Second Chances in Cheshire Bay
Unforgiven in Cheshire Bay
Flirty in Cheshire Bay
Up to Date listings can be found on my website.
www.hmshander.com

Acknowledgements

Ten, people, TEN! This is my tenth public thank you in the back of a book—I'm so thrilled to have made it this far, there are tears of happiness in my eyes as I write this. Although writing a book is a mainly solo endeavor, I could not have this ready for you to read if not for the cheerleading and support of some magnificent people in my life.

First – my Shander family, whom you may know on my social media platforms as Hubs, The Teen, and Little Dude. Thank you for allowing me to toss out ideas into the air, to write while you played your three-hour long games of Shadows or Gloomhaven, and for asking me what my daily word count was. Thank you for encouraging me to keep going and to chase my dreams, and for the nonstop coffees I sometimes needed when I was on a role. I love you all with my whole heart.

To my parents and in-laws and extended family – Thank you for your support, endless cheerleading, and encouraging your friends and family to give my books a try. Having you visit me at markets and book signings means the world. I have an amazing family, and every day I'm thankful to you all. Thanks for being you.

To my wonderfully dedicated alpha reader – Mandy. As soon as those first chapters are written, you are my go-to person. You let me know what works, what isn't, and if those opening lines, pages and chapters are enough to hook a reader into wanting more and I'm so appreciative of that. It's great having you to bounce an idea or two (or a couple hundred) and you are such a fantastic mentor and cheer squad. I heart you more than you'll ever know.

To my beta readers – Arlene R., Josephine H.,

Lacey K., Lana V., Nicole S., and Roxy K. Thank you for spending your free time reading my words and pointing out what didn't make sense and what needed to be expanded on, and how much you enjoyed Tess and Jon. Your critiques were as welcome as your enthusiasm. It's great having you in my corner and I hope you'll want to read the next MS I have sitting in the wings.

To my cover designer – When that first image came in, my mind was blown. You pretty much nailed my vision, and you captured the essence of the story. I'm so thrilled we worked on this together, and I look forward to many more covers designed by you.

To my editor – Irina. A change from the rush that seems to be our normal, this time you got a couple of extra weeks. Thank you for putting in the editing time, for meeting the deadline and highlighting where things should be improved to make the character a little stronger. Camille's story will be harder and more intense.

To my proofreader – Krista. You rock! Thank you so much for your hard work, for being ahead of schedule and for your comments. It warms my heart that Jon may have become your new favourite book boyfriend. Looking forward to using your services in the future.

If I missed you, it certainly wasn't intentional. I know I couldn't be where I am without the help of so many others. Thank you! And thank you for reading and making it all the way to the end. You all rock.

About the Author

H.M. Shander is a star-gazing, romantic at heart who once attended Space Camp and wanted to pilot the space shuttle, not just any STS – specifically Columbia. However, the only shuttle she operates in her real world is the #momtaxi; a powerful electric car that transports her two kids to school, work, and various sporting events.

When she's not commandeering Elektra, you can find the elementary school librarian surrounded by classes of children as she reads the best storybooks in multiple voices. After she's tucked her endearing kids into bed and kissed her trophy husband goodnight, she moonlights as a contemporary romance novelist; the writer of sassy heroines and sweet, swoon-worthy heroes who find love in the darkest of places.

If you want to know when her next heart-filled journey is coming out, you can follow her on Twitter(@HM_Shander), Facebook (hmshander), or check out her website at www.hmshander.com.

Manufactured by Amazon.ca
Bolton, ON